Something cracked. The railing gave way, and Shell screamed. Ryler grabbed her arm and jerked her toward him.

They landed in a heap by the door with her face buried in his solid chest. She pushed away from him.

He helped her up. "You okay?"

"Fine. Thanks."

The balustrade where she'd stood was gone, leaving twisted, splintered wood in its wake.

Yellow pollen dust smeared her pink T-shirt and jeans. She swiped at it with shaky hands, and managed to pat most of it out.

Ryler coughed and cleared his throat. A few gasps later, he caught his breath.

"Are you sick?"

"Allergies. All this pollen. If it's green and grows in the spring, I'm allergic to it."

"And you're a landscaper?"

"Gotta make a living somehow." Ryler ran a hand through his dark waves, sending them tumbling in disarray.

Shell swallowed hard.

"I don't remember you having allergies before." But she remembered everything else. His deep voice that sent shivers over her spine, his touch that shot lightning through her veins, and his kiss that turned her into a quivering, brainless idiot.

SHANNON TAYLOR VANNATTER is a stay-at-home mom, pastor's wife, and writer. When not writing, she runs circles in the care and feeding of her husband, Grant; their eight-year-old son; and their church congregation. Home is a central Arkansas zoo with two charcoal gray cats, a chocolate lab, a dragonfish, and three dachshunds in weenie dog heaven. If given the chance to clean house or write, she'd rather write. Her goal is to hire Alice from *The Brady Bunch*.

Books by Shannon Taylor Vannatter

HEARTSONG PRESENTS
HP902—White Roses
HP921—White Doves

White
Pearls

Shannon Taylor Vannatter

Heartsong Presents

To Mama, for being the unique individual you are, for encouraging my dream and helping me achieve it. You instilled in me a love for reading, helped me go to all those writers' conferences, and babysat so I could meet deadlines.

Acknowledgments: I appreciate Jeannie Webber from the Little Rock, AR, Children's Home Administration Office, Carrie Korzen and Tina Thomas of the Rose Bud Post Office, and Nick Stark, owner of the Darden-Gifford House in Rose Bud.

A note from the Author:
I love to hear from my readers! You may correspond with me by writing:

Shannon Taylor Vannatter
Author Relations
PO Box 721
Uhrichsville, OH 44683

ISBN 978-1-61626-223-5

WHITE PEARLS

All scripture quotations are taken from the King James Version of the Bible.

All of the characters and events in this book are fictitious. Any resemblance to actual persons, living or dead, or to actual events is purely coincidental.

Our mission is to publish and distribute inspirational products offering exceptional value and biblical encouragement to the masses.

PRINTED IN THE U.S.A.

one

Great, just what Shell needed to spoil the view from the balcony. A church full of Holy Rollers across the street. At least the old plantation sat back off the road a good two hundred yards. The Bible-thumpers wouldn't be able to spy on her. With an exaggerated eye roll, she ran her forefinger and thumb back and forth over the faux pearl necklace she wore.

She stood at the railing and surveyed the grounds of the crumbling, two-story relic. Transform this place into a happening bed-and-breakfast? On the edge of town in tiny Rose Bud, Arkansas?

But the place had charm. It had obviously once been a grand estate. Oh the balls and cotillions this house must have hosted. Oh the grand, fine ladies who'd lived here. Grand, fine ladies who looked down their snooty noses on the likes of Shell Evans.

"Shell Evans." A hoarse male voice came from behind her.

She stiffened. Probably a carpenter. How did he know her name already? She'd barely gotten here. Already the gossiping tongues wagged. *Wade Fenwick's floozy is in town.* She could almost hear the whispers. Paranoid. Of course, her boss had told the man her name.

"Who wants to know?" She smiled, trying to sound confident as she turned to face him.

Ryler.

Her jaw dropped. Her heart skittered into overdrive. Her knees turned spongy and she leaned back against the railing.

"The landscaper."

If only this could be an April Fool's joke.

A massive brick of a man—but she knew how gentle he could be. Despite his imposing size, he was easy to look at. Same model-worthy, sculpted bone structure with tousled

5

dark waves almost brushing his shoulders, and haunting moss green eyes. Eyes that bore into her soul and seemed to hold all of life's hurts in their endless depths.

Hurts she'd once tried to ease. Instead she'd almost lost her heart. "Darrell hired you?"

Something cracked. The railing gave way, and Shell screamed. Ryler grabbed her arm and jerked her toward him. They landed in a heap by the door with her face buried in his solid chest. She pushed away from him.

He helped her up. "You okay?"

"Fine. Thanks."

The balustrade where she'd stood was gone, leaving twisted, splintered wood in its wake.

Yellow pollen dust smeared her pink T-shirt and jeans. She swiped at it with shaky hands, and managed to pat most of it out.

Ryler coughed and cleared his throat. A few gasps later, he caught his breath.

"Are you sick?"

"Allergies. All this pollen. If it's green and grows in the spring, I'm allergic to it."

"And you're a landscaper?"

"Gotta make a living somehow." Ryler ran a hand through his dark waves, sending them tumbling in disarray.

Shell swallowed hard.

"I don't remember you having allergies before." But she remembered everything else. His deep voice that sent shivers over her spine, his touch that shot lightning through her veins, and his kiss that turned her into a quivering, brainless idiot.

"It was fall. I'm good in fall and winter. I'm usually better than this, but I forgot my medication last night." His gaze scanned the grounds. "This place has a lot of possibilities."

"It'll take a lot of work, but it's doable." The porch swing beckoned to her still wobbly legs, but she didn't trust the rotting wood and rusted chains. "You know, I'd understand if you want to back out of this. I'm sure you can find another job." *Please do. Just walk away.*

"Probably, but we're both adults. I'm starting my own

business and something as upscale as restoring the grounds of a former plantation will look great on my résumé." He coughed and cleared his throat.

She hugged herself and managed a smile. "Whatever you think."

"I think I've seen enough." No returned smile, no handshake, no catch ya later. He strolled through the doorway and was gone.

Why? Why? Why? Of all the landscapers, why the one who'd almost made her believe happily-ever-after could be possible. Six months. A whole half a year without him. Yet one glance and her heart had done a giddy tap dance.

Darrell stepped through the doorway. "What happened?"

"I leaned against the railing."

His eyes widened and he gently took her by the shoulders. "Are you okay?"

"Fine."

He wagged a finger. "No leaning on anything until the carpenters do some work."

"I thought you said it was structurally safe."

"In 1982, a tornado hit Rose Bud." With a shrug, Darrell checked his watch. "Some of the outbuildings got blown away, but the house survived. Just think of the history. Famous architects of the time, DeVoss and Carr designed it for the original owner, J. S. Darden."

"When did you get here?" Shell's frustration came out in her tone.

He raised an eyebrow. "Just a few minutes ago."

"I must have been inside opening windows. It needed airing out."

"We parked around back by your apartment."

"You mean my slave quarters." She rolled her eyes. "Leave it to you to buy an old plantation and house me in the slave quarters."

Darrell laughed and his brown eyes almost closed like they always did when he smiled. "Actually the servants' quarters are upstairs. There's a separate stairway from the dining room. And technically since the house was built in the late-1800s, they were no longer slaves, but servants. But think of all the history. When I saw it for sale, I had to have it. It'll be fun restoring this place back to its original glory."

If only his unconcerned, worry-free attitude could make her forget Ryler's presence. But her nerve endings were alive at the prospect of working with him. "Is this an April Fool's joke?"

"Wish I'd thought up something." Darrell snapped his fingers. "But I forgot what day it was. Seriously, I wish I could oversee this renovation project myself, but then I'd miss my lovely wife."

The only upstanding, happily married man Shell had ever known, Darrell was one of the few she was sure would never hit on her. He and his wife, Eva, were the stuff romance novels were made of.

"You have to admit it's beautiful." Darrell strode to one end of the balcony. "Ryler's here somewhere. The landscaper."

"I sort of ran into him."

"Good. He's planting a garden on all four sides with a fountain in the middle of each."

"You said three months, Darrell? This place will take at least six, maybe even a year. I'll never get to go home again."

"Three. Maybe six if we hit snags, definitely not a year." Darrell framed the front yard with his hands. "Just imagine. A garden view from every window. Freshly painted siding and new glass in the broken windows, restored interior walls and flooring. . ."

The breeze blew pollen dust tornadoes across the long drive.

"Darrell, I'm not sure about this." Three months—six months. Either way, too long. What was she doing here anyway? Why wasn't she with Chance in Conway? "It's a bigger job than I expected."

"You have my blessing to go home every weekend to Chance if you want. And there's a church right across the street if you decide to stay here."

"You know I don't do church, and I'd rather spend every evening with Chance." She bit her lip.

"I can't keep up. How old is he now?"

"Fifteen months."

"You could bring him here with you."

She closed her eyes. "You know that's not possible."

"Nothing's impossible. You could stay on, run this place for me, and raise Chance here."

Except she couldn't raise him.

"Come on, Shell. This place needs your touch."

And she owed him. "Three months. That's all I have to give."

"That's my girl." He patted her shoulder. "So now do you see the potential?"

"It's a great old place." *It's the landscaper that's the problem.* "Three months, then I'm out of here."

"That's all I need. But think about what I said. This little town would be a great place to raise a child." Darrell checked his watch. "I've got a meeting to get to. I'll come back tomorrow for an official tour and we'll go over the plans. Will you close the windows and lock up for me?"

"Sure."

"You can whip this place into shape, Shell. I have complete confidence in you."

The only person who ever had.

Without a backward glance, he left. Moments later, his black cherry Cadillac convertible rounded the house. With a wave, he drove away.

Slinging her purse over her shoulder, she hurried through the house and retraced her steps, closing windows as she went.

The musty smell was better than when she'd first arrived. She closed the last window, locked the storm and regular doors, and stepped out on the front porch.

"Guess I'll see you tomorrow."

Shell jumped and whirled toward the gravelly voice.

"Sorry, didn't mean to startle you."

"I thought you left."

"I was checking out the grounds." He jammed a baseball cap on his head and tipped it at her. Dark waves flipped every which way under the rim. "Better get used to me hanging around. You're stuck with me, for at least six weeks."

Only half the time she'd be here. A relieved sigh welled up within her, but she stifled it as he waved and jogged toward the back of the house.

Moments later, a charcoal SUV rounded the side of the house and pulled onto the highway. If it was Ryler's, it was definitely a step up from the battered royal blue pickup with the roaring engine he'd driven six months ago.

Her breathing leveled out to normal.

The splintered railing lay in front of the steps. Her stomach clenched. She could have ended up there in a broken heap. Picking up the rotted wood, she threw it in a pile next to the porch and scanned the house.

Six weeks. Six weeks of working with Ryler. The crew could whip this place into shape in three months. They had to. She had to get home to Chance.

Inhaling the fresh spring air, she tried to let the peaceful surroundings calm the quaking inside and imagined the repairs, flower beds, and bushes. Yes, it definitely had potential.

A breeze wafted the tall, amber hay surrounding the house on three sides. Dense woods stretched into eternity behind her apartment separate from the house. Typical of rural Arkansas, hayfields surrounded almost every house, although downtown Rose Bud was just around a curve.

The porch spanned the entire front, with filigree trim and the balcony above it. The window with stained glass panels Darrell had bought in Botkinburg graced the eave overhanging the terrace. His only splurge from keeping everything original. So excited with his antique find, he'd had the window installed months ago when the roof had been replaced and the apartment remodeled.

Double French exterior doors would be perfect for the front entries on both stories, but Darrell wanted the originals with the double arched windows left intact.

Her purse vibrated. She dug out her cell and flipped it open. Darrell.

"Hello?"

"You okay?" Darrell's favorite Christian radio station played in the background.

"Fine. Why?"

"You seemed kind of—funny, so I wanted to make sure you weren't hurt."

A lump lodged in her throat. "It wasn't the fall. I wasn't expecting to see Ryler here, so it kind of rattled me."

"You know him?" Concern echoed in his tone.

"We got acquainted when he was working on the golf course."

"And that's all you're going to tell me." The music faded out. "He did wonders with the golf course, so I thought he'd be perfect for the job. But you're giving me second thoughts. Will you be okay working with him?"

"It's fine. He's gone already and what are you? My boss or my father?"

"Just trying to look out for you, Shell. Somebody needs to. Have you made it to the apartment yet?"

"On my way."

"Call Eva when you get there. She's dying to know what you think."

"I'm sure it will be fabulous. Even if it's not slave quarters."

He chuckled. "Take care, Shell. And if Ryler gets out of line, he can answer to me."

Her heart was the only thing out of line.

As she hung up, a child's giggle echoed through the air, followed by a playful squeal. Now she was hearing things. Painful reminders.

She turned toward the sound. A mother with a toddler and an infant walked toward the house across a narrow hayfield. Great, just what she needed.

Scurrying to her apartment, she rounded the side of the main house. With a screened porch on the side, and a small afterthought of a porch over the door, the back of the main house wasn't nearly as ostentatious as the ornate front.

Separated from the house by the driveway, her apartment sat directly behind it, with an aged wooden garage on the far end. Its door looked permanently jammed about a foot from closed. She shuddered. No telling what kind of creatures had made their home in there.

Coffee. Darrell promised her apartment was fully furnished and stocked with everything she'd need. Two cups, maybe three, then she'd go over the plans and blueprints and be ready for Darrell's arrival in the morning. And Ryler's.

She opened the trunk of her car and pulled out the largest suitcase, then sifted through the keys Darrell had given her.

So much for slinking into town without a splash. Who was she kidding? This job would take forever. No way could she spend months on end here without the locals finding out who she was. Six weeks of those months on end, working with Ryler.

Oh well, at least she wouldn't have to hear her sister and brother-in-law constantly talking about God and church and inviting her to attend.

The aged lock of her temporary lodgings clicked. Inside, the apartment was roomy with sunny yellow walls and white wicker furnishings. Eva had done a nice job with the contemporary, bright, and cozy decor. Given the chance, Shell would have chosen a less hokey color, but it was nice enough. And after Shell finished the job, it would serve as a nice honeymoon suite.

She stepped into the bedroom and hoisted her suitcase onto the bed. After unzipping the lid, she dug through her clothing, found the framed photo, and set it on the night table. She ran her fingertips over the precious face, her chin trembling.

Weekend trips to Conway. Lots of them over the next several months. Home was only forty-five minutes away and she'd left something there.

Her heart.

And the only male she'd ever trusted with it.

☙

Ryler parked in front of the glass lobby of the post office. If he'd known the manager for the B & B project was Shell, he wouldn't have taken this job. He should have known. Shell was never far from Darrell. White-knuckled, his hands tightened on the steering wheel.

But she was supposed to be in Conway. And now, he couldn't quit—couldn't let her know that working with her would be hard on him. Hard on his heart.

How had she gotten back under his skin so quickly? He jerked the SUV door open.

She was beautiful, but he'd had his share of beautiful women. Was it the pain in her eyes that had drawn him to her again? He didn't need to dabble with anyone else's pain—he had enough already.

Pushing thoughts of Shell down deep, he concentrated on the task at hand. Meeting his sister. Shortly after his birthday, he'd finally found the courage to unearth his mother's letter from his father's Bible, read it, and head to the bank with the safe deposit key. And his life had pole-vaulted even more out of control.

He'd found his birth mother but hadn't revealed his identity to her yet. Her highfalutin ways made him want to run the other way. Until he learned about his siblings. Siblings who possibly didn't even know about him.

With his stomach churning, he stepped inside the post office lobby and swung the second door open to reveal white walls and commercial tiled floors. Mailboxes lined a long wall and several U-shaped areas. The work area was to his right.

He blew out a breath. She was alone.

Turning from her computer, Laken flashed him a friendly smile. "May I help you?"

His tongue glued to the roof of his mouth. He swallowed. "I just moved to Romance."

"Welcome. I used to live there. It's a great little town."

"I'm trying to decide whether to get a post office box there or here in Rose Bud, since I'll be doing some work in this area, Searcy, and Little Rock."

"Hmm." She tapped her chin with her index finger. "It depends. Is the Romance office close to your house?"

With a shrug, he grinned. "Beats me."

"Where do you live?"

"In a rental house on Highway 5."

Squinting, she cocked her head to one side. "By any chance is Pete Callaway your landlord? Number 124?"

He frowned. Was she on to him? "How did you know?"

"I used to live across the street. My brother lives there now and he mentioned someone new moving in." She shrugged. "Besides, it seems everybody ends up in one of Pete's two rentals when they first come to town."

Across the street from his brother? He couldn't have planned that if he'd tried.

She grabbed a scrap of paper and drew an X, then a line and another intersecting it. "Okay, your house is here. The office in Romance is down this road, I'd say about a mile and a half past your place."

Ryler tried to concentrate on her directions. "It's not on the way home either way."

"We can set up a box here or my husband can help you at the Romance office, or you might want to put up a mailbox at your house."

"Your husband works at the Romance office?" Married? Was he an uncle?

"He's the postmaster there. I used to work there, too, but as things developed, I transferred." She blushed.

Her coloring was different from his. Her hair a coppery brown, while his was quite a bit darker, a shade or two from black. Her eyes were blue, while his were green. But there was something about her smile. Something he'd seen in the mirror.

She frowned, obviously uncomfortable under his scrutiny. "Maybe you should check with my *husband*."

Did she think he was hitting on her? Ryler grinned. "I'm sorry. I didn't mean to stare. You seem familiar to me."

"I had the same thought about you. Are you from around here?"

"I've lived my whole life in"—he hesitated, considering a lie—"Little Rock." Would she figure it out? Did he want her to? Did she even know he existed?

"I used to live in Little Rock. Maybe we ran into each other there." She visibly relaxed then snapped her fingers. "I know. You were working at my parents' home a few months ago. Martin and Sylvie Kroft in Searcy. I'm Laken Winters."

His gut clenched. "You have a good memory. Ryler Grant."

She'd waved to him and he'd ignored her, assuming she and the man with her were just another pair of snooty visitors and she had been doing her good deed of the day by acknowledging the hired help. Only later did he learn from the Krofts' young, flirty neighbor that they were Laken and Collin Kroft—he had a sister and a brother.

"I think I'll go ahead and get a box here." The perfect way to get to know Laken without her knowing who he was.

"Sure." She handed him a form. "Just fill this out. You can do it now or take it with you if you want." She rattled off the box sizes and prices.

He'd better go before he got her suspicious again. What if she heard he'd been asking around town about her? "I appreciate your help. I'll be back tomorrow."

"Have a nice day." She turned back to her work.

Forcing his feet to move, he headed toward the lobby.

Shell strolled in, her platinum hair blowing in the slight breeze. A strand fell across her eyes. His fingertips tingled, longing to brush it away from her face. Of all the leggy blondes he'd known, this one was dangerous. He should have taken her offer. Reneged on the job and run as fast as he could. Far away.

"Hello again."

"Hey." He stepped back out of her way.

Her flowery-citrus perfume filled his senses. The perfume

he'd bought her. He'd thought he caught a whiff of it at the soon-to-be B & B but decided it was his imagination. But no. She was definitely wearing the perfume he'd bought her. What did that mean?

"Shell Evans?" Laken cried.

Her nearness sank into his bones.

"Laken Kroft."

"Winters now. I got married last February."

"Don't tell me." Shell rolled her eyes. "Married in Romance on Valentine's Day."

"Guilty." Laken laughed. "What about you?"

"I've never married."

Ryler swallowed hard.

Both women looked at him, as if wondering what he was still doing there.

Spying. That's what. On both of them. He laid the form on the counter and grabbed the pen waiting there. "I decided since there's not much to it, I'll fill it out here."

"What about you, Ryler?" Laken raised an eyebrow.

He cleared his throat. "What about me?"

"Are you married? Any kids?"

Typical happily married female. She'd just met him and was trying to fix him up with her buddy. She didn't know his heart had already experienced Shell Evans and never recovered. "Nope. I guess y'all know each other."

"Laken and I went to the same school in Searcy." Shell's laugh dripped sarcasm. "Though in decidedly different circles."

"I never paid any attention to circles." Laken smiled.

"My boss, Darrell Norton, set up a P.O. box for me." Sarcasm gone, still Shell's frigid tone could chill a cold-house rose. "I'm supposed to pick up the key."

"Sure." Laken bent to search under her counter. "So, let me introduce y'all."

Ryler concentrated on filling out the form, as if he wasn't listening to their conversation.

"Too late. My boss hired Ryler to transform the grounds at

the Darden-Gifford House. We're renovating it into a bed-and-breakfast."

"Oh, I've always loved that place." Laken handed her the key. "What kind of work do you do?"

"I'm supposed to be an apartment manager, but when my boss has a new project going, I play remodeling supervisor and interior decorator, too."

He gripped the pen tighter until his fingers turned white. Darrell was never far from Shell.

Turning toward the exit, Shell waved. "I'll see you around, Laken. And, Ryler, I'll see you bright and early."

As the door closed behind Shell, Laken propped her elbows on the counter. "She's pretty, isn't she?"

Ryler swallowed but couldn't find his tongue.

"She's not married—you're not married."

He held both hands up, palms facing her. "I'm not looking to get married."

"I don't think she has a very high opinion of herself."

"Why? She's gorgeous."

Laken pointed at him. "I knew you thought she was pretty."

He cleared his throat and handed her the completed form. "On that note, I think I'll go."

"Hang on. Here's your key." She handed it to him.

"Thanks." He hurried out.

Yes, Shell was as beautiful as she'd ever been.

And Darrell was still part of her picture. He'd always seemed overly concerned for her when Ryler had worked the golf course in Searcy.

Had things progressed between them? Was Darrell housing his mistress in Rose Bud?

What did it matter? Things with Shell were long over. But his bruised heart didn't know it yet.

And right now, he needed to concentrate on the Krofts.

❧

"You taking up residence up here?" Darrell's voice came from behind Shell.

Standing a few feet from the balcony railing, she inhaled a

deep breath but didn't turn to face him. "It's peaceful."

And on this project, she needed lots of peace.

"Just don't lean on the railing again." Darrell tucked Shell's hand in his elbow. "Let's officially tour this treasure."

That being-watched feeling crept up her spine. Her gaze canvassed the lawn.

Ryler's stare bored a hole through them as he squatted amidst a pile of rocks and potting soil.

Shell turned away and opened the door. With the musty smell carried away by the breeze, she inspected the house more thoroughly. Propping her chin on one fist, she surveyed the landing flanked by twin bedrooms with plank walls and floors. A few bits of aged wallpaper and scraps of dingy newspapers covered the walls, with glimpses of insulation between the wood.

"The closets line an entire wall. We'll cut them in half and expand out to install a bathroom in each room."

Ugly metal flues jutted from the wall in each room. "Please tell me you don't plan on putting in woodstoves."

"I'd like to, but it wouldn't be very feasible. Central heat and air work much better."

"We could find black iron potbellied stoves with electric logs for looks."

"Now you're getting a feel for the place."

Sheetrock and carpet would get this place in order. But Darrell wanted the house restored, not remodeled.

"I want the original wall planking sanded, and the cracks between each piece of wood filled. At some point there was paneling, which left all the nail holes. Those will have to be filled, too, and then the natural wood can be polyurethaned."

A fresh coat of neutral paint would save the wide, baby pink baseboards. The paneled walls in the landing could be stripped to their original wood, leaving more nail holes and cracks to fill.

Darrell opened the door opposite from the balcony to reveal narrow steps. Flipping on the light, he gestured her ahead of him.

Shell climbed to the attic. The long room boasted the fancy window above the balcony. "Plenty of room to add a closet and another bath."

"I figure the only bathroom downstairs in the entry can serve as a communal powder room for all guests, but we'll need another for the staff."

She ticked off each one on her fingers. "How many bathrooms do you plan to add?"

"Three upstairs, one in the attic, one in the downstairs bedroom, and one for staff. Space won't be a problem since each room is rather large."

No. Just time.

A fast plumber. Was there such a thing?

Oh, why had she let Darrell talk her into this project?

Because if not for Darrell and Eva, Shell might have ended up like her mother.

"That's all up here." Darrell ushered her in front of him.

Shell led the way down from the attic and down the main staircase.

The lone bedroom downstairs was the largest. Plenty of room for the proposed bathroom. She strolled through the spacious, once fancy living room.

"See the transom windows over the doors? All original for circulation. The fireplace is original, too."

The blackened fireplace needed to be torn out and replaced, but Darrell would never agree. She continued into the dining room with the large bay window and faded white wainscot and into the large kitchen with ancient cabinets.

"We'll cut off part of the pantry for a staff bathroom. The original pump is out on the screened porch." Darrell opened a door off the dining room to reveal a narrow stairway.

Servants' quarters. She climbed the passageway to a bedroom. With no hallway, she had to walk through the first room to get to the second identical one. Scraps of newspaper covered the walls in the second room. Squinting, she made out a date: February 1, 1890. Closets lined the dividing wall in each room, back to back.

"Why are there newspapers on the walls?"

"To keep the wind from blowing through the cracks. They didn't have insulation back then. It was blown in later."

Shell shivered. "Glad I didn't live back then."

"You're definitely not the rough-it type." Darrell grinned. "There's really no way to put in a hallway, so this will be a suite. This first room will be a sitting area. The closets are back to back, so we'll take part of both for the bathroom, and expand out into each room a bit. The second room will be the bedroom."

"It all sounds doable. You've thought of everything."

"So how are the Chance withdrawals?"

She swallowed hard. "Doable. Barely."

"Tell me again why he's not with you."

"You know why."

"I've heard your reasons, but as much as you love him, he should be with you. You're his mother."

"Savannah is his mother."

"She's his aunt. You're his mother."

"She's his legal guardian. Why can't you see he's better off with Savannah and Jake? This way, he's got a good life with two stable parents." *Without me. Without the specter of his father.*

She descended the stairwell, retracing her path to the front entryway. Halfway through the living room, a hand clamped over her elbow.

Gently, Darrell turned her to face him. "I just don't—"

The front door opened and Ryler stepped inside the foyer.

Her breath caught.

Darrell let go of her.

Ryler cleared his throat. "Darrell, when you get a minute, I need to compare notes with you on the fountains."

Not wanting to get any closer to Ryler, she turned sideways to let Darrell pass. "You go ahead. We're done."

"I'm meeting Eva for lunch, so I'll have to head back to Searcy soon."

"It won't take long." Ryler backed out and Darrell followed.

Blowing out a deep breath, Shell hugged herself. Close encounters of the Ryler kind.

&

The balcony beckoned and Shell stepped out the windowed door. Standing in the middle, away from the railing, she listened to the constant squeals and giggles from the steady stream of toddlers next door. She hugged herself. Next door wasn't just a house. It was an in-home day care.

Day two of trying to avoid Ryler. All morning, she'd directed carpenters, picked replacement glass, and chosen a just-right white paint for the siding. Several men on scaffolding surrounded the house, measuring, prying rotted wood, sanding cracked paint, and scraping old caulk from window frames.

Her gaze kept drifting to Ryler as he unloaded sack after sack of potting soil and mulch. He heaved another bag and the muscles in his arms rippled. Oh, the feel of those arms around her. She shivered. It would have been easier on them both if he'd had his products delivered in bulk, but Darrell didn't want enormous piles in the carpenters' way.

After dumping his load in the pile near the house, Ryler turned and caught her eye.

Busted.

He pushed dark chocolate waves out of his face. "When you get a chance, I need you to choose plants and tell me where the beds will go."

"I don't know a thing about plants."

"No problem. I do."

No grin, no expression. The most animated she'd seen him so far was yesterday at the post office. Did he have a thing for married women? Or was it only Shell he shut down with?

"Can you come up here?"

"Sure." He grabbed something from his truck and jogged toward the house.

Working side by side with Ryler, picking plants, edging, and fountains. Would she be capable of rational thought as they hovered over catalogs, their heads huddled close together, while her heart leapt around like a giddy teenager? *He's just a man.*

Within minutes, he strolled out onto the balcony and shoved a catalog at her. "This will help. I'll need you to choose what kind of edging you want, too. I like using lots of native rocks throughout the beds. It gives a masculine look and not all B & B visitors will be women."

Don't think about how his hand almost touched hers just then. "Good point. What about water fountains? Darrell wants one on each side of the house."

"They're in the back of the catalog. Who's that?"

Shell looked up from the catalog and he gestured toward the long drive leading to the house.

A couple crossed the street. The man carried a casserole dish and a plant, while the woman pushed a stroller.

Great, shove a baby in her face. Shell rolled her eyes. "Probably the welcoming committee from the church."

"Pack of do-gooders."

At least they were like-minded on one issue. "I wish they'd stay on their side of the road."

"Me, too, but we better make nice. They could be potential customers."

By the time Shell and Ryler made it downstairs, the couple was almost to the porch.

Shell got a better look at the woman and stifled a gasp.

two

"Welcome to Rose Bud." The man set the plant on the porch rail and stuck his hand toward Ryler.

Luckily this rail was sturdier than the one upstairs.

The two men shook hands.

"Miss Evans, I'm not sure if you'll remember, but I'm Pastor Grayson Sterling and this is my wife, Adrea."

Grayson Sterling? Sara Sterling's husband. A chill crept down Shell's spine. The last time she'd seen him, they were nine and she'd dubbed him the preacher's brat.

"Hi, Shell, it's good to see you." Adrea smiled. "We brought you a plant from the floral shop. I hope you like white tulips."

Beneath all her sweetness and light, accusation dwelled in Adrea's gaze.

Killed with fake kindness by the woman whose fiancé Shell had once stolen. She wasn't sure she had the stomach to play this game. Mustering up a fake smile, she took the terracotta pot. "Thank you."

"You can plant them this fall if you like." Adrea gestured toward the dish. "Grayson's sister is a caterer, so she made the sandwiches. There's enough for the entire crew. Probably tomorrow, too, if you keep them refrigerated."

Ryler frowned. "Don't we need to pay you?"

"Not at all." Grayson waved away the suggestion. "Sis catered a big wedding last night and brought us a few leftovers."

"We'll certainly put them to good use." Ryler grinned. "Much obliged."

"I've always loved this place." Adrea surveyed the house. "So, you and your husband are overseeing the work?"

"We're not married." Shell and Ryler echoed one another.

"Oh." Adrea blushed.

"I'm the landscaper. Ryler Grant. Shell lives in the apartment. By herself."

Awfully intent on having nothing to do with her other than work.

"I'm so sorry. I saw you both up on the balcony and assumed. . ."

"We were discussing beds." Shell's tongue tangled. "I mean—flower beds."

"How fun. I own the floral shop in Romance, so, Ryler, if you'll stop by, I'll give you my wholesaler's card. They're very reasonable."

"Great. Hey, maybe you could help Shell with your flower knowledge."

"That's not necessary." Shell swallowed. Adrea's brand of perky set her teeth on edge.

"But you don't know a thing about flowers and if Mrs. Sterling helped, I could concentrate on the fountains, edging, and soil."

Less time spent together. And get this job done quicker. But working with Adrea? Or Ryler? Adrea? Ryler? Adrea?

"I'd love to help." A wail emerged from the stroller and Adrea scooped the baby up, a poof of pink ruffles, a shock of dark hair, and an angry red face. She nuzzled in her mother's arms and calmed. "Unfortunately, it's almost time for Ashley's nap and then I have errands to run. I'm working the rest of the week, but I could stop by early next week."

"Perfect. We'd really appreciate it."

"I love big old houses." Grayson scanned the balcony. "I heard the apartment used to be slave quarters."

Shell mustered up a tour guide smile. "I thought the same thing, but the house was built after slavery was abolished and the servants' quarters are upstairs. Apparently, the apartment was built later than the house."

"Are you remodeling the apartment, too?"

"It's already done on the inside and when we finish the transformation, I'll move out so it can serve as the honeymoon suite."

"How romantic." Adrea turned a dreamy-eyed gaze toward her husband. "Maybe it'll be finished in time to spend our next anniversary here."

Shell suppressed a gag.

"Maybe." Grayson kissed her temple, then the baby's, and tucked Adrea's fingers in his elbow. "Oh, almost forgot. We're having a yard sale the last Friday and Saturday of this month to benefit the Arkansas Children's Homes. We've got nice things people donated. Furniture, artwork, dishes. You name it, we got it."

"I might have to check out the dishes." Ryler grinned. "I'm tired of paper plates."

"Good, maybe we'll see you then." Grayson patted Adrea's hand. "We're also having a Mother's Day picnic over at the church next month."

A knife twisted in Shell's stomach. She'd never get to celebrate Mother's Day. "I'll have to check my calendar."

"Y'all are welcome to come and my sister's helping with the food, so you won't want to miss out." Grayson listed all the various services and times at the church. "If you don't have a church home, give us a try."

With a wave, he pushed the empty stroller down the drive as Adrea cooed to the tiny bundle she held.

"So, how do you know them?"

"It's a long story." A sordid one.

Something crinkled. Shell turned to face him.

A wad of aluminum foil filled the empty spot in the container. Ryler's sandwich already had a bite missing. "Mmm, I'm starving."

"I'll tell the other guys before you eat them all." She grabbed a sandwich for herself and rounded the house.

Scaffolding framed the side with several men at various heights. She cupped her hands around her mouth. "Lunch is on the porch, guys."

The foreman started down his ladder. "I brought mine. I didn't know lunch was part of the pay."

Shell didn't answer. Ryler could explain. She just wanted

the quiet of her apartment.

Careful not to scuff her heels, she tiptoed across the gravel drive. So, Adrea ended up married to the preacher whose wife Wade killed. And they had a baby. Both of them came out just fine after Wade literally wrecked their lives.

A smirk played across Shell's lips as she remembered sneaking up behind Wade, wrapped only in a towel, and the horrified expression on Little Miss Goody-Two-Shoes' face.

Entering the apartment, she hurried to the kitchen. Ice clanged from the dispenser and diet soda fizzed as she poured it into the glass.

Memories chased one another and her smile faded away.

With a shudder, she hugged herself. She hadn't been to see Wade since his mother put him in the nursing home in Searcy.

Why did women like Adrea always get happily-ever-afters while Shell ended up alone? Not that she wanted a preacher—just the happily-ever-after part.

How many demons from her past could she face in one day? A child's laugh echoed through the open kitchen window. Her demons were laughing at her.

A loud *whir* started up outside, signaling that the men had inhaled lunch.

She took a bite of the sandwich. Chicken salad and it was probably really good, but her taste buds were dead.

❧

Ryler sank onto the foot of the bed. His bed, but the rental certainly didn't feel like home. He hadn't had a home since he was eighteen. The drab white walls closed in around the queen-sized bed that almost filled the room, leaving barely enough room to turn sideways and walk around it.

He looked toward the ceiling, rolling his head from side to side. Tense muscles and tendons popped and ground against one another in his neck and shoulders. Ill at ease at home— ill at ease at work.

She hadn't worn his perfume in four days. Instead she'd worn a light, powdery floral scent. Proof that she hadn't worn his perfume that first day because she missed him but because she liked the smell.

Maybe having Adrea help Shell with the flowers would keep her at a safe distance. The more he saw her, the more he wanted to beg for another chance.

But he'd never been the begging kind and Shell Evans wouldn't drive him to his knees.

He opened the third drawer of the dresser and pushed his T-shirts aside. It was still there. The envelope with the deposit slip and statements from the bank. Twenty thousand dollars earning interest in his account.

What kind of person left that kind of cash lying around in a safe deposit box for thirty years? Guilt? Love? Regret? He ran his hand through his hair.

Never had he held that much money. It would come in handy with building his company.

Maybe having struck out on his own would impress Shell and she'd reward him with a flirty smile. But it would mean nothing. All of her smiles were flirty.

Possibilities brought a grin to his lips as he remembered how soft she felt against him when she literally fell into his arms. Who knows, maybe another fling would get her out of his system. A nice distraction while he checked out the Krofts.

What if Laken and Collin weren't worth knowing any more than Sylvie was? He'd move on. With no ties to bind, no roots, it didn't matter.

Carefully, he put the envelope back in the drawer and covered it with clothing.

No. He'd sworn off women. The last thing he needed was Shell dallying with his heart again until she got bored and cast him aside. No more women.

But why did she have to come in such an attractive package?

A knock sounded at the door. Ryler slammed the drawer shut. Who could that be?

He hurried to the door, picking up a stray sock and remote

on the way and stashed them behind a throw pillow on the couch.

A young boy in a wheelchair greeted him, with Collin standing behind.

Ryler's jaw dropped. Who was the boy? Maybe he had a nephew.

"I'm Collin Kroft and this is my son, Brady. I live across the street." Collin gestured a thumb in that direction. "Thought we'd introduce ourselves to the new neighbor."

You mean your brother. Do you know about me?

Collin frowned. "Maybe now isn't a good time."

"Ryler Grant." He offered his hand and Collin shook it.

"Welcome to the neighborhood. Let me know if you need anything."

"And if you like to play basketball, I do, too." The boy grinned.

"I'll bet." Ryler smiled.

"I'm really good." Brady rolled his chair back and forth in quick succession. "I play on a wheelchair league in Little Rock."

Why was Brady in a wheelchair? A lump lodged in Ryler's throat. To be so young and confined to a chair.

"Well, we won't keep you. Let's go, Brady. Ryler's probably busy."

"Actually, I'd like to see you shoot a few hoops, Brady. I could use a break from unpacking." Ryler held up his index finger. "Hang on a second."

He hurried inside and scooped the basketball from the closet then sprinted back outside.

"There's a hoop in the back."

"Cool." Brady rolled himself around the back of the house. From fifty feet away, he lobbed the ball through the air with perfect spin and arch. *Swoosh.* Nothing but net. If there'd been a net attached to the rusty hoop.

"You're very good." Ryler leaned against the back porch. "Are y'all from around here?"

"I grew up in Searcy, lived in California for the last several years, and moved to Romance a few months ago to be close to Brady."

Divorced and the boy apparently lived with his mom. "I met your sister at the post office today when I got my box and she told me you were my neighbor."

"Laken's a gem. What kind of work do you do?"

"I'm a landscaper. You?"

"I'm a comptroller at a fragrance company in Little Rock." Collin leaned against the porch beside Ryler, crossing his arms over his chest. "Are you working steady?"

Ryler nodded. "I worked on a golf course in Searcy, and I actually worked on your folks' place a few months back. Your sister remembered seeing me there."

"I knew you looked familiar. So, why settle in Romance?"

"I like the area." Ryler kicked at the gravel. "Right now I'm working the grounds of a B & B in Rose Bud."

Brady effortlessly swished another goal.

"I heard Shell Evans was heading that up." Collin smirked. "The old Darden-Gifford place."

"You know her?"

"Half the guys in Searcy know her, if you know what I mean," Collin whispered.

Ryler's throat constricted. His hands fisted. How well did Collin *know* Shell? Why did it bother him to hear her talked about that way? Because there was something vulnerable about her. Used and discarded. Just like him. Only she'd discarded him, too, so why should he care?

"I shouldn't have said that." Collin cleared his throat. "She may have changed. Lord knows I have. Or have I? Sometimes I wonder. I became a Christian a few months back. Unfortunately, there's a lot of the old man left inside of me, but I'm working on him."

Okay, don't have a clue what you're talking about. Even though his adoptive parents had taken him to church, the more Collin talked, the more confusion clouded Ryler's brain. *What old man?*

"I've got an early commute in the morning, so I better get

Brady home. He's got exercises to do and we haven't eaten supper yet. Want to 'bach' it with us? My sister sent over a pot of veggie soup."

Tempting, but he'd had enough sibling exposure for the day. "It sounds great, but I better get back to unpacking."

Collin clapped his hands to be heard over the constant thud of the dribbling basketball. "Come on, Brady. Let's go."

"Bye, Mr. Grant." Brady passed the ball to him.

"Bye, Brady. Come play ball again some time and please, call me Ryler." *Uncle Ryler? Uncle Martin? Martin Kroft Jr.?*

They disappeared around the side of the house. Ryler went in the back, stashed the ball in the closet, and sank into the couch, cupping his head in his hands.

He'd officially met both of his siblings now. Still, he only had questions.

Why had Sylvie thrown him away, but kept Collin and Laken?

His father's Bible sat on the coffee table. Riley Grant, the only father he'd ever known. Flipping near the middle, he found the letter. Carefully, he unfolded it.

Dearest Ryler,

If you're reading this, it means your father and I are in heaven. We can't bear to think of you all alone. I'm sorry, son. We should have told you about the adoption all along, but we were selfish, and afraid that if you knew, someday you'd try to find your biological family and leave us. We hope this news isn't too jarring. Just know that we couldn't have loved you more if you were our own.

Please, son, find your family, with our blessing. Your birth mother left the safe deposit key at the children's home. In the safe deposit box, you'll find twenty thousand dollars, a letter from your birth mother, a strand of pearls she wanted you to have, and trust fund papers. Please use the money to open your adoption records and claim your inheritance. For your future.

Your loving parents,
Riley and Loretta Grant

He traced his fingers over the precise scrawl. Could he trust her words? His mother had been the ultimate optimist. She could put a sweet spin on the worst disaster. She'd probably had complete faith that Ryler would come home. Right up until her last breath.

He closed his eyes.

Could he trust Sylvie? Trust the woman who gave him away at birth? Trust the woman who lived in her upscale neighborhood while his adoptive parents struggled to keep food on the table and never touched the stack of bills now padding his bank account?

He refolded the letter and set it back inside the Bible. A yellow streak on the page caught his eye. A verse his father had highlighted.

"Trust in the Lord with all thine heart; and lean not unto thine own understanding."

ஃ

With each car that neared, Shell tensed from her perch on the balcony.

Six fifteen. Any minute perky Adrea would show up with flower advice. Maybe she'd forget. Not a chance. Women like Adrea kept their word.

A silver G5 sports car turned into the winding drive. The perfect little perky car for perfect little perky Adrea.

Blowing out a sigh, Shell closed her eyes. She cut through the landing and marched down the stairs, sidestepping carpenters, tools, and lumber. The constant *whir* of production rang in her ears.

As Shell opened the front door, Adrea stepped up on the porch.

"Listen." Shell propped her hands on her hips. "You don't have to do this. I can muddle through the catalogs and Ryler can give me any flower info I need to know."

"But I'd really like to help. I'm excited to be in the planning stage of such a large undertaking."

This woman couldn't be for real. No one was that nice, that happy. "I haven't had the chance to check with my boss. I can't guarantee a consulting fee."

"I'm not here for money. I just love gardens."

Shell stifled a sigh. "Let's just get it out in the open. I know you hate me." With just cause.

"I don't hate you." Adrea grinned. "Okay, there might have been a time when I did. But that was another lifetime ago. I brought you white tulips. Do you know what they symbolize?"

"I'm not much on flowers." Shell cocked an eyebrow. "That's why you're here, remember?"

"I knew it was you overseeing the restorations here before Grayson and I came over last week."

Shell's mouth went dry. "How?"

"News travels fast in a small town. I purposely brought you white tulips because they symbolize forgiveness."

"Forgiveness." Shell's tone symbolized sarcasm. "You think I need forgiveness."

"I wanted you to know that whatever happened between us is in the past—I don't hold it against you." Adrea clasped Shell's hand. "And if I did anything that hurt you, I hope you'll forgive me."

Pulling her hand away, Shell swallowed hard. Adrea couldn't be blamed for anything.

"Mrs. Sterling." Ryler jogged around the side of the house. "Great timing. I have the garden plans. Ready to get started, ladies?"

⁂

Shell's heart ached for Chance, even though she'd spent the last two weekends with him. To have those plump little arms around her neck.

Sitting cross-legged on the balcony with landscaping plans surrounding her, she couldn't focus. If only Savannah and Jake had agreed to officially adopt Chance. Then there would be closure. Like this, Shell could reclaim him anytime. Savannah and Jake even encouraged her to. And Darrell.

Chance was better off without her. Without Wade Fenwick's shadow haunting him.

And to top everything off, there was Ryler. She tried to ignore him working below. Ignore the muscles bulging under his shirt, ignore the impressive expanse of chest, ignore those intense eyes.

How could a man who spent so much of his time playing with flowers be so manly?

Think about the project. So far, the plumber was amazingly fast. Soon the bathroom fixtures would be in place and the framework for the walls would go up. The crew showed up daily, working hard and steady. Already, the house looked better, though most of the grounds were covered with fresh dirt.

"Hey."

So much for not thinking about Ryler. She looked down from the balcony.

"I picked up something extra from the wholesaler. Come see what you think."

Frowning, she hurried through the landing and down the stairs. They'd gone over Darrell's budget. There wasn't room for anything extra.

Standing by his truck, he motioned toward the bed. "What do you think?"

A pristine, white porch swing sat in the back of his truck, surrounded by scalloped terra-cotta edging and stepping-stones.

"I've seen you staring at that porch swing. Since you seem to spend most of your time up there, I thought you could use a perch in your makeshift office."

Sweet gesture. But what did he want in return? "It's beautiful. But the budget. . ."

"The wholesaler gave me a deal on the edging since I bought so much, so I used the difference on the swing. It can go back if you don't want it. But I figured future guests could enjoy it."

"You're right. Definitely keep it."

"The guys will need to replace some boards on the ceiling, but they can have it up in a few days. I'll get this unloaded and make another trip for the first load of plants."

Movement in the drive caught her attention. The preacher again. Shell rolled her eyes.

More food, but at least Mrs. Perky and the wailing baby weren't with him.

"Lasagna anyone?" Grayson held two trays stacked on top of one another.

"Mmm." Ryler hurried down the drive.

Reluctantly, Shell followed.

"My sister catered a dinner party last night. Most of her well-to-do clients don't do leftovers, so Grace ends up with extra food."

"You really shouldn't bring everything here." *Can't you just stay on your side of the road?* "Think of all the hungry children in China."

"I took most of it over to the homeless mission in Searcy. My secretary heated these up for y'all."

Shell's mouth clamped shut and she took a dish. "Thanks. The men will love it."

"I wanted to remind y'all about the yard sale Friday and Saturday. And the picnic next Saturday. We really want y'all to come. Your whole crew."

No way. She planned on spending Mother's Day weekend with Chance. And even if she wasn't, there was no way she'd spend it with a bunch of Holy Rollers.

"We'll see." She set the dish on the porch and headed to her apartment. "Lunch, guys," she shouted. "I'm going to get plates."

Drills and saws stopped buzzing. Men descended ladders and scaffolds and hurried to the porch.

"Y'all are all invited to a picnic at the church next Saturday. My sister's helping with the cooking."

Shell ducked into the safety of her apartment, tempted not to go back, but she had to take the crew plates to eat on.

She knew how the religious nuts worked. Come to our yard sale. Come to our picnic. Suck people in and make them feel obligated. Then before they knew it, they were in church. She'd fallen for it as a kid and her mother had let her go.

Anything to get Shell out of her hair.

Shaking her head, she focused on steeping the cold brew tea bags in the pitcher.

But Shell wasn't good enough for church either. She didn't fit in. The church kids' parents didn't want their little angels hanging with the likes of her.

"Do you know who her mother is?" Sylvie Kroft's whispers echoed through the entire congregation.

A tap sounded on the door. "Hey, need some help?"

Her chest tightened. Her home. A boundary Ryler had never crossed, even during their relationship.

"Um, sure. Come on in." She stacked paper plates, napkins, and plastic forks on the table.

His huge frame made her living room seem small. Masculinity overtook everything despite the feminine, flowery decor.

"If you can take these, I'm in the process of making sweet tea real quick."

"Now you're talking." He grabbed the stack of paper products but paused in the doorway to her bedroom.

Crossing another boundary. "Excuse me?"

"Sorry. Couldn't help but notice what a neat freak you are. I never even make my bed and you've got everything just so. How long does it take to arrange all those frilly little pillows?"

"I like my surroundings neat." The only thing she could control. She had to get used to seeing him daily, without her heart threatening to flutter out of her chest. Become immune to him. If that were possible. "After work, would you like to come by and have coffee with me?"

"Having coffee was how it all started with us." Knifelike words delivered in a stone-cold tone. "This time around, let's keep it business only. Just business."

Even though he'd misunderstood, his rejection stung. "Exactly what I had in mind. Listen, I don't like being uncomfortable around someone I work with. So, I thought maybe we could become friends."

"Friends?" He frowned. "I guess we could give it a try."

"Good. I'm tired of the tension." Sucking in a relieved breath, she removed the cold brew bag from the pitcher. She dissolved the sugar in hot water and dumped ice in.

Grabbing Styrofoam cups, she carried the pitcher out, only to have Ryler take it from her.

The men stood in a pack around the lasagna, ready to pounce.

Ryler stuck two fingers in his mouth and delivered an ear-splitting whistle. "Hey, ladies first. She made us sweet tea."

No one had ever called Shell Evans a lady. It sounded kind of nice. Except that Ryler knew she wasn't a lady. And he wanted nothing to do with her.

ॐ

Ryler entered the post office. Laken pushed aside a stack of envelopes, ready to wait on customers. The *whir* of the air conditioner kicked on.

"Hey." She flashed him a genuine smile. "I'm glad you stopped in today."

"Lots of mail?"

"No. I wanted to ask you something." She disappeared for a moment, then handed him three envelopes. "Hayden and I are having a few friends over for dinner Saturday night and we wanted to invite you. You can bring a date if you want."

The perfect chance to spend time with her and meet her husband. "What's the occasion?" He sifted through his mail.

"Just newlyweds settling down after three months and having our first dinner party. Actually, a backyard barbecue."

"Let me guess. You invited Shell and you want me to round out the twosomes?"

"I said you could bring a date." She grinned. "And I told Shell the same thing."

His gut sank. "Is she bringing anyone?"

"I don't know. Why don't you ask her? She might agree to be *your* date."

He pointed at her. "I knew you were up to something."

"Who me?" She shrugged innocently. "Collin and his new

lady will be there. I haven't met her. Have you?"

"Aha. This whole thing is actually a setup to get your brother to bring his lady friend to meet you. And it's less pressure on him—and her—if you have several people over."

She propped her hands on her hips. "How'd you get so smart?"

"Let's just say I've dealt with a few women in my life. I know how they think." Except Laken seemed different. Could her motives be pure?

"So, will you come?"

"Sure. Sounds great."

Spending time with Shell would cost him. Especially if she brought a date. But spending time with his sister—priceless. "See ya then."

"Do I need to bring anything?"

"Just Shell." She grinned.

Shaking his head, he left. Why not? Maybe he'd ask Shell—since they were friends and all. Who was he kidding? No sane man would want to be friends with Shell. Still if he asked her, then he wouldn't have to deal with her showing up with a date.

Seven miles of highway passed while he rehearsed asking her.

As he pulled into the drive, the words still weren't flowing.

Shell stood in the front yard, inspecting a truckload of glass as the workers carefully unloaded it. Her plunging neckline held everyone's attention. Despite his gaze riveting on the shadowy depths, he wanted to tell the rest of them to keep their eyes to themselves.

She signed off that nothing had arrived broken or damaged. Reluctantly, the workers returned to their jobs, and the truck pulled away.

Staring at her clipboard, she turned toward the house.

He cleared his throat. Now or never. "Shell."

"Hmm." She stared at her clipboard for several more seconds before looking up.

Forcing his gaze to stay on her face and not drift downward, he swallowed. "Are you going to Laken's Saturday night?"

She scrunched her nose. "I don't know. I'm not sure why she asked."

"I think she's just being nice, trying to help us not feel like such outsiders."

"But she and I weren't really friends growing up. I mean— she lived in a nice neighborhood and I lived in a trailer park." She frowned. "She invited you, too?"

"I thought we might go together."

"Together?" One eyebrow lifted.

three

"Unless you have a date?" Ryler's insides twisted.

The power tools buzzed to life. The compressor hissed, followed by the *ka-thwack* of a heavy-duty nail gun. Shell jumped. "What happened to just business? They might think we're dating or something."

"Just trying to implement that friends thing you mentioned, and I've never been one to care what anyone else thinks. Besides, I think Laken was trying to set us up."

Shell's fingers tightened on the clipboard. "Really?"

"Now, don't go getting all mad. This way, she'll give up. If we come together and she sees there's nothing going on, she'll chalk us up as just friends. Which is what we are." *Yeah, right.* "Besides, I hate walking into a place where everybody knows everybody, and I don't know a soul."

"I guess that would be okay." Turning her attention back to her clipboard, she hurried to the house as if she couldn't wait to get away. But she'd said yes.

Spending time with Shell, under the guise of friendship. What was he thinking? All he wanted to do was rekindle their past relationship. To kiss her, hold her, and love her. But she was done with him. Maybe spending time with her in a working relationship and as a friend would be better than the last several months without her.

Or pure torment.

⌘

Shell scanned her wardrobe. Nothing without a plunging neckline. And he was business only. Then why had he asked her to go with him? Did he really want to be friends? She hadn't meant real friendship—just an easy working relationship.

Not that it mattered. She pulled out a sleeveless purple blouse, and buttoned it higher than usual, then wiggled into her least faded jeans. Turning a circle in front of the mirror, she evaluated the outfit. Not come hither, but not dowdy either. She slipped on her favorite low-heeled gold sandals. As she finished her look with gold hoop earrings and a matching necklace, she heard the crunch of tires on gravel.

On second thought, he might be all business, but let him struggle with the view. She undid the top two buttons and grabbed her purse. Sprinting out to meet him, she slowed to a walk. *Don't appear too anxious.* The only thing she was anxious about was getting this evening over with. Why had she agreed to go?

Because deep down, she hoped to surpass "just business." To reclaim what they'd once had. To let her guard down and allow herself to love him. To know he loved her in return. But stuff like that didn't happen in real life. Not in hers, anyway.

"Hey." She climbed into the truck.

His gaze stayed firmly on her face. "Glad you could make it."

A prick of disappointment jabbed her stomach. Was he really immune to her charms? And why did it bother her so much for Ryler not to be interested anymore? She'd broken up with him. He was her past. Not her future.

He pulled onto the highway as silence vibrated between them. Flicking on the signal, he turned left at the intersection.

"If I got my directions right, the house isn't very far after Doc Baker's veterinary clinic. We should be getting close. I bet that's it." He pointed to a rustic house with a long porch across the front and a ramp leading up to it.

Several vehicles were already in the drive. Who were the other guests? Shell had been so preoccupied with one particular guest, she hadn't really thought about the others.

They got out of the truck and strolled toward the house. The door opened and a man she didn't know greeted them.

"You must be Ryler and Shell?" The man extended his hand. "Hayden Winters, Laken's husband. Glad y'all could make it. Everyone else is already out back."

Hayden ushered them into the cozy living room with

dozens of family photos displayed on the walls. They followed him through the kitchen, equipped with unusually low cabinets, to the sliding glass doors.

A large deck spanned the back of the house, and it had a ramp similar to the one in front. Charcoal and lighter fluid flavored the air. Shell scanned the group already there. Adrea, the preacher, and Collin Kroft. Her heart lodged in her throat. A redheaded woman, a man she didn't know, and a vaguely familiar brunette woman.

Laken's gaze lingered on Shell's blouse for just a moment. "I'm so glad y'all made it."

Shell stiffened as Laken greeted her with a hug.

"This is Shell Evans and Ryler Grant. You both know my brother, Collin."

Too well. Complete, total jerk.

"This is his friend, Jill. Andrea and Grayson said they'd met y'all. Now this part gets complicated." Laken gestured to the sandy-haired man. "Mark is Grayson's associate pastor and Adrea's brother. His wife, Grace, is Grayson's twin. Shell, you probably remember Grace from school and when we attended Thorndike."

Grace. How could she have forgotten?

A round of hellos and nice-to-meet-you's echoed through the crisp spring air.

So, Grayson had followed in his father's footsteps and Grace had carried on the tradition by marrying a preacher.

Great, dinner with not one but two preachers.

Hmm. Scurry to the bathroom and make clothing adjustments or give them a little test. See if these Bible-thumpers could keep their eyes aboveboard. Shell smirked.

"So, Shell." Collin's lips pursed, forming a thin line, and he kept his gaze on her face as he handed her a red plastic cup. "I hear you're overseeing the work at the old Darden-Gifford place."

"When we finish, it'll be a happening bed-and-breakfast."

He turned to his redheaded companion. "Jill is an architect. She'd love the place."

"Oh, how nice." Small talk with Collin grated on her nerves. But the Collin she knew couldn't possibly be any more comfortable than she was with the two preachers. That knowledge brought a smile to her lips.

"I need some big strong men to move the picnic table off the deck to the yard." Laken clapped her hands to be heard above the chatter. "And some ladies to help carry all the fixin's outside."

All of the women trickled inside, but Shell didn't hurry to help. She wasn't a lady and surely Laken had enough assistants. As the men tackled the table, Collin stayed by her side.

Her insides twisted as she sipped from her cup. Sweet tea.

"You know. . ." He ran a hand through his hair. "I owe you an apology. I treated you badly in the past."

She choked and spluttered.

"You all right?" Ryler called.

With a cough, she retrieved enough breath to respond. "Fine."

Collin sighed. "You're worth much more than you realize, Shell. Don't sell yourself short."

Her eyes stung. "You don't know anything about me," she snapped. "What? Are you a preacher now, too?"

"No, but I did become a Christian a few months back. Obviously, I've got a long way to go, but I'm trying to be a better person."

The low moan of a dog's howl echoed in the distance. A symphony of barks and yaps joined in.

She turned away and watched the men heave the table into place.

Thankfully, Ryler came to her rescue. "You sure you're okay?"

"Fine, my tea just went down wrong." She linked her arm through his, grateful for his presence.

With a confused frown, Ryler turned to Collin. "Where's Brady tonight?"

Clearing his throat, Collin's gaze flew to an approaching

Jill. "He's staying with Hayden's parents."

"Who's Brady?" Jill threaded her fingers through Collin's. His jaw clenched. "My son."

Jill's eyes widened. "You have a son? You're divorced?"

"Actually, we never married."

"I guess you planned to tell me all this at some point?" Jerking her hand out of Collin's grip, Jill crossed her arms over her chest. "I think I'd like to go now."

Jill stalked around the side of the house, with Collin and Laken scurrying after her.

Laughter bubbled up inside Shell. Any minute, she'd lose the battle.

※

Ryler felt for Collin, but if he didn't want trouble with his date, he shouldn't have hit on Shell. His own brother's date. But Collin didn't know that part.

His stomach twisted. What kind of man was Collin? What kind of brother?

He'd certainly gotten a rise out of Shell. Had they been involved in the past?

What kind of family was this? Ryler ran a weary hand through his hair. What he wouldn't give to be able to sneak inside and check out all those family pictures he'd seen in the living room. Were there any of Martin Kroft Sr.?

"Hey. Where'd you go?" Shell elbowed him.

"Nowhere."

"There for a minute, I'd have sworn you were in another galaxy."

"I guess I didn't expect you to know almost everyone here. I guess y'all went to school together?"

"Unfortunately."

"What's Thorndike?"

"The church in Searcy, where Grace and Grayson's dad preaches." She gazed off in the distance, obviously distracted by memories. A smile tugged at the corners of her lips, but a frown marred her forehead. "I attended for a short time. So did Laken and Collin."

Didn't see that coming. Shell in church?

"Did Collin say something to upset you?" *Nice way to ease into it.*

"Actually he apologized for something that happened a long time ago." She sighed. "Something best forgotten."

"Let me guess." Ryler's teeth clenched. His insides tightened and heat scalded his airways. "He broke your heart."

Her sarcastic laughter crackled with tension. "No. But he wanted to. I was dating his best friend and Collin made a play for me."

His hands balled into fists. Why did Collin's audacity make him so angry? Ryler didn't have any claims on Shell. He didn't want any claims on her.

Or did he?

Ryler worked at keeping his tone even. "Not hitting on your buddy's girl is an unspoken rule between friends."

"Collin sort of went by his own rules."

"But he apologized. Seems kind of odd." Why did he feel so protective of her? At the beginning of their relationship, he'd set out to use her just as Collin had.

"Says he's a Christian now." She rolled her eyes. "He gave me this big song and dance about how he's changed, but I'm not falling for it."

Laken rounded the side of the house. "Two guests down. So much for our first successful party."

"It wasn't your fault." Hayden drew her to his side. "Burgers are ready. Who wants cheese?"

At least Laken didn't play any games. He grinned. Other than matchmaking anyway.

❧

Ryler pulled into his driveway and killed the engine. Though he'd already dropped Shell off, her perfume still lingered in the cab.

The black Lexus sat across the street at Collin's.

Despite the warning flares in his veins, Ryler jogged over.

The porch light illuminated Collin sitting on the top step. "Know anything about woman troubles?"

His brother—the traitor. He'd better be talking about Jill.

"I guess I complicated things for you tonight."

"It's not your fault. I should have told Jill the truth. But how do you tell a woman you care about that you're a failure?"

He cared about Jill. Not Shell. "You're a comptroller. I wouldn't say you're a failure."

"In my personal life, I am. I was too cowardly to marry the love of my life. After I left, Katie learned she was pregnant and had our son. Alone." Collin huffed out a big sigh. "Then she got sick and wrote me a desperate letter, but my new girlfriend hid it for three years. It's a long story, but in the meantime, Katie died and her brother, Hayden, had to step in and raise the son I didn't know I had."

Collin had followed in their mother's footsteps and abandoned his child. Was it a family tradition? At least he hadn't knowingly abandoned Brady. "That's pretty deep."

"Try living it." Collin ran a hand through his hair.

"We've all done things we're not particularly proud of, but I've seen you with Brady." An itch drew Ryler's attention to his arm. A mosquito. He smacked it. "He's crazy about you."

"I've only been in his life about a year and he still lives with Laken and Hayden during the week."

Why? Not up to the challenge of raising a special needs child? Ryler shrugged. "You're repairing things with him. That's honorable. And if Jill's not interested in kids, that's her problem."

"She loves kids, but I wasn't honest with her. She's big on honesty, and at the moment, she's not taking my calls."

"If you really care about her, go to her place." Another mosquito buzzed his ear and he swatted it away. "Don't leave until she lets you explain. The least she can do is hear you out."

"You're right." Collin stood. "A shrink would charge for that kind of sound advice."

"It's on the house."

"What's up with you and Shell? Are y'all seeing each other?"

"We just work together. She didn't have a date and I didn't either, so we came together."

"That's all there is to it?"

Unfortunately. Ryler nodded.

"In case things change, I'm sorry for what I said about her. She seems different than she used to."

"Trust me. Nothing's going to change." No matter how badly he wanted it to. With a wave, he jogged back across the street.

The tensed muscles in his shoulders relaxed. At least Collin wasn't interested in Shell.

&

As the workers carefully popped the old glass out of an upstairs window, Shell held her breath. Showers of glass rained down from the scaffolding despite their caution, and thankfully none of the men stood underneath.

"You should stay farther back until they finish." Ryler spoke from directly behind her.

Her breath caught. She didn't turn to face him. Three weeks of working with him and his nearness still snatched her breath away. "I wish you wouldn't sneak up on me like that."

"I was afraid some of the glass might hit you and tried to rescue you, but I didn't make it."

"I don't need rescuing."

"Hello?" a cheery voice called.

Shell groaned. She'd recognize that voice anywhere. Sylvie Kroft, Laken's mother, the biggest busybody on the planet.

With a sigh, Shell turned around. Sylvie still wore her hair too red and her lipstick too bright. Gems graced almost every finger. Real, no doubt. Less made up, she might have been an attractive woman.

"Sylvie?" Shell forced her lips into some semblance of a genuine smile. "To what do we owe this pleasure?"

Sylvie's mouth shaped into an *O*. "Why, Shell Evans, as I live and breathe. You're all grown up and pretty as a picture."

Shell frowned. A compliment? What was Sylvie up to?

"I just took some of Grace's leftovers to the homeless shelter and Meals on Wheels, but Pastor Grayson wanted me to bring these sandwiches over."

Sylvie and good deeds. It didn't compute.

Her too-red eyebrows drew together. "You're the young man who worked on my lawn a few months back."

Ryler's jaw clenched. "Yes, ma'am."

"I heard something about this place being turned into a bed-and-breakfast." Sylvie handed a tray to Ryler. "Such a grand old place. I'd have liked to have seen it in its day."

Be nice to a potential customer. Shell shrugged. "Maybe you will. The owner is restoring it according to original photos."

"I'd love to get a tour sometime."

What game was Sylvie playing? She cleared her throat. "Maybe when more work is done. Right now, it's rather an obstacle course."

Although, it might be fun to invite Sylvie to the balcony and encourage her to lean against the railing.

"Mr. Grant will do a marvelous job here." Sylvie clasped her hands together. "I can't wait to see this place in all its former glory."

"Well, we appreciate the sandwiches. I'll go grab something to drink and tell the crew." Shell rushed toward her apartment.

"I best be getting on my way," Sylvie called. "Bye, dear."

Shell managed a stiff wave. Dear? Since when had Sylvie Kroft called Shell Evans anything besides trash?

❧

Ryler trudged to his bedroom and fished the large, black velvet box from the third drawer. Flipping it open, he stared at the pearl necklace then dumped its contents on the bed. With trembling fingers, he unfolded the letter for the hundredth time.

Dearest Marty,
    Your father and I never wanted to give you up. Please use the money to find us.

The pearls have been passed down through six generations. Only part with them if you must.

The letter went on, but he'd never been able to read any further. Uninterested in her excuses, his gaze scanned to the end.

Martin and Sylvie Kroft
Searcy, AR

He traced his fingers over the long, slanted, flowery signature. Just like she'd signed his check for the yard work he'd done a few months ago.

His hands fisted, half-wanting to wad the note and rip it to shreds. Instead, he refolded it, careful to follow her original creases, then he tucked it back in the lid of the box, with the trust fund papers in the name of Martin Rothwell Kroft Jr.

Martin Kroft. Marty Kroft.

He'd never laid eyes on Martin Kroft Sr. But the Krofts' young, flirty neighbor had spilled everything she knew. Martin Kroft—his father—was a hermit. And an alcoholic.

Trust fund? How much? It didn't matter. Money definitely didn't equal happiness. His adoptive parents may have struggled financially, but they'd been wealthy in love and happiness. Until his graduation. Until they'd told him he was adopted. The night he'd been so angry, he'd left and never gone back.

Until three days later, after they died in a house fire.

Scooping up the necklace, he rolled the perfect, polished pearls between his callused thumb and forefinger. Were they real? A jeweler would know. He hooked both hands through the strand and pulled in opposite directions. Break the string and watch them fall. Show Sylvie Kroft what he thought of her heirloom. But, if they were real, it would be a shame to destroy them.

Releasing the tension on the necklace, he replaced it in the box and closed the lid, with a spring-loaded final *snap*.

Half a dozen people milled around as Ryler surveyed yard sale items under the huge oak tree beside the church.

He stopped in front of a large painting. A waterfall surrounded by rocks and greenery. So real, he could almost hear the water splashing.

It could almost quell the storm brewing in his soul after yesterday's close encounter with Sylvie Kroft. He sucked in a deep breath and let it seep out slowly. *Don't think about her.*

An elderly man tried to dicker with one of the workers.

"All proceeds go to the Arkansas Children's Homes," Adrea called.

Exactly why he'd come, since he'd spent the first weeks of his life there. But he'd also needed to clear his head. And escape Shell. Just get through the morning, then he'd have a nice long break since she planned to go home for the weekend again.

Even back when they were seeing each other, she'd always run off to Conway every weekend. What kept dragging her there? A man? No, surely she hadn't cheated on him. Maybe her family lived there. People who cared? People she cared about?

Scanning the glassware, video cassettes, and books, he tried to rid his thoughts of her. Lamps, trinkets, and stuffed animals lined numerous tables with clothing racks sagging beneath their loads.

Why did he care? He couldn't give her the opportunity to use her feminine allure to tie him in knots and then cut him loose again.

Seeking peace, he strolled back to the soothing painting.

"That's just down the road." The familiar voice came from his left.

He looked up then did a double take.

Sylvie Kroft stood beside him. Her green eyes, so like his own, bore into Ryler. "The Romance Waterfalls in the painting. They're real and quite lovely. You should go sometime."

"Maybe I will." His throat muscles tightened. Tell her soon or flee?

"Even though it's a print, it's a ridiculously good buy."

"Yes, ma'am." His jaw clenched. Hug her or spit in her face?

"The flower beds you planted are just starting to bloom. You did an outstanding job."

A compliment? Before, she'd only barked orders and complained. "Thank you, ma'am."

"What are you doing in Rose Bud?"

"I like small towns."

"Mother, are you done?" Laken's voice came from behind him. He turned to face her.

Laken smiled. "Thinking of buying it?"

"Just admiring."

"My friend got married there a few years back, so her father painted the original and made copies for all her wedding attendants. This one was mine."

"Why is it here?"

Laken rolled her eyes. "They're getting a divorce. She didn't want the original anymore, but she couldn't just throw it away since her father painted it. So, she gave it to me and I donated my print to the church."

"Honestly, young people these days." Sylvie sighed. "The slightest difficulty or argument and they're off to see the divorce lawyer."

"All too true." Laken checked her watch. "We need to check on Father. Nice to see you again, Ryler."

Was something wrong with their father?

"You two know each other?" Sylvie wagged a finger between him and Laken.

"I met your daughter at the post office."

"Little wonder. She practically lives there."

"Are you coming to the picnic next Saturday?" Laken tucked her hand in Sylvie's elbow.

"I've been invited." But he'd stick out like a sore green thumb.

"Then you should come. Meet some more people and the food is always great."

"We'll see."

"Hope to see you there." Laken waved and the two women headed to Sylvie's white Lincoln.

Was it his imagination or had Sylvie's attitude come down a peg or two since he'd worked for her? Though she had enough money to set up trust funds, she didn't live in a mansion. Yet she'd strutted around the two-story as if it were a grand palace.

Laken didn't put on any airs. Since she once lived across the street from his rental house, obviously status wasn't important to her. Was there a trust fund for her, too? If so, would it change her? If Ryler let them know who he was, would the money change him? Did he even want it? Did he want them?

"I saw it first." Shell's voice came from his right.

He turned to face her, and his chest did that weird quivery thing it always did when she was near. Her white jeans showed all her curves and they were topped with the plunging neckline of a yellow blouse. Her blond hair was pulled high in a neck-baring ponytail, revealing huge silver, hoop earrings. Why didn't she realize she'd be just as eye-catching in an enormous, shapeless housedress like Aunt Ginny wore?

"Saw what first?"

"I'll take it." She pointed at the painting.

"I believe I saw it first," Ryler deadpanned. "But you're in luck. I was just looking."

"Good. It would be perfect above the bed in my apartment. I mean, in the honeymoon suite. Oh, but I'm not sure I could leave it there. I may buy it for myself."

A yellow-and-black-striped butterfly flitted about the white flowered bush beside the church, giving him something to look at other than her. "I hear it's a real place over in Romance."

"I better go pay for it before somebody else snatches it up."

"I'll take it to the apartment for you."

"Wonderful. Thanks." She pulled a key off her chain. "I

have a spare. Stick it and the painting inside the front door for now. I'm on my way out of town."

"Sure." He loaded the painting in his truck. Tempted to stay until she left, just to be near her, he started the engine instead. *Lovesick sap.*

Away from Shell's appeal, Ryler drove across the street, forcing himself not to glance back at her in the rearview mirror. Gravel crunched under his tires as he traversed the long driveway, circled around behind the big house, and parked between it and the apartment.

Ryler unlocked her door and slid the painting inside. As unwieldy as it was, she'd never be able to hang it herself. He jogged to his truck and dug out the necessary tools.

Back inside, he hesitated before entering her bedroom. Was he invading her privacy? No, he was doing a nice thing for her.

Yet during their three-month relationship, she'd spent countless nights with him, but never invited him to her place. What did she have to hide?

Whatever it was, it was none of his business now.

He spread a clean drop cloth over her headboard and fancy pillows. Propping the painting on the headboard, he checked for studs, then moved to the foot of the bed and eyeballed it. Centered perfectly and on studs, too. That didn't happen very often.

After slipping off his work boots, he stepped up on the bed. Holding the painting with his knee, he drove a screw into the wall. The gun jerked as the screw bit into the stud. He slid the large landscape into place.

Again, he stood at the foot of her bed to make sure it was still centered. Perfect. Carefully, he folded the drop cloth over without spilling any of the dust, took it outside, and shook it. Back inside one final time, he smoothed her flowery bedspread and made sure the numerous pillows were still in place.

The frame on her nightstand caught his attention. A toddler dressed in blue. Who could he be? Obviously, someone very important to Shell. Ryler's chest tightened.

Did she have a new man in her life? A new man with a child looking for a mother?

&.

Sunday evening, Shell let herself in the apartment. Already, she missed him. Every time she went home for the weekend, Chance had grown, learned new complicated words, and discovered new foods. And she was missing all of it. Who was she kidding? Even at home, she missed all his firsts.

She rolled her suitcase to the bedroom, dumped the dirty clothes out by the hamper, and sorted the laundry into three piles. A good shove sent the suitcase under the bed, and she started out to get the laundry basket.

The waterfall painting hung over her bed. She stopped in midstride. Just where she'd wanted it. Only Ryler could have hung it there.

Her gaze flew to the picture on her nightstand. Her stomach jolted.

Maybe he hadn't noticed.

And even if he had, Chance could be anyone to her. A nephew. A friend's child. Her heart.

Gently, she picked up the picture, kissed her fingertips, and pressed them to his cute toddler grin. Her vision blurred. Only an hour ago, she'd held him and experienced his drooling kiss. How could she miss him already?

&.

Shell waited for Ryler to notice her. But he didn't.

On his hands and knees, he placed large boulders around the fountain and scattered about among the greenery, rosebushes, and blooms. Though each rock was placed just so, it looked natural when he finished.

"Ahem."

He sat back on his heels and turned to face her.

"Thanks for hanging the painting for me. It's exactly where I wanted it."

"I was hoping you wouldn't get mad at me for going inside when you weren't home."

"No, I appreciate it."

"Originally, I slid it inside the door, but then I thought about how bulky it was and I just didn't see how you'd ever be able to hang it by yourself." He pushed a stray wave out of his face. "How was home?"

"Fine." Her voice quivered. "I really didn't want to come back here."

He looked down, almost as if her admission hurt him.

No, she was imagining things.

His eyes squinted and his face contorted with a sneeze, then another, and another.

"Bless you. You forgot your allergy pill again?"

"No, it just hasn't kicked in yet." He fished a tissue from his pocket and swiped at his reddened nose.

Cute Rudolph impression.

"Did you plan on going to the church picnic Saturday?"

"On Saturdays I go home."

Ryler winced. "I hate to be the bearer of bad news."

"What?" Her teeth clenched.

"The foreman said the heat-and-air guy called to say he can come Saturday to do the estimate, or it'll be two months before he's free again."

"Two months?" She stomped her foot. "We can't wait two months. We need to get the work done way before then." Her tone registered high and panicky.

"I told the foreman I thought you'd want the guy to come Saturday, so he arranged it."

Her shoulders slumped. "So much for home."

"I suggested you'd probably prefer him to come as early as possible. He said it would only take a few hours and the foreman arranged for him to be here at ten, so maybe you can still go."

Another sweet gesture. Why? His green eyes shimmered in the sunlight. And why did he have to look so good?

"And I was thinking." He shrugged. "After he consults with you, he can do the inspection while we're at the picnic."

She frowned. "Why do you want to go to the picnic so badly?"

"I don't. But I was thinking if we go, the preacher might leave us alone."

A heavenly thought. "Good thinking. And, Ryler, thanks."

"For?"

"For getting the heat-and-air guy to come early. I really need to be home this weekend." She might not get to actually celebrate Mother's Day, but at least she'd be with Chance.

"No problem." His gaze swept past her. "Speak of the devil."

Shell turned to see Grayson coming down the drive, holding two foil pans.

A heavy sigh escaped her. They had to get rid of him. Maybe attending his picnic would do the trick.

❧

Purposefully, Shell had picked the too-short shorts to wear to the church picnic to see if the Holy Roller men could keep their eyes off her legs. Most of them could, but a few stole a quick glance, then looked away. The older women's mouths puckered in disapproval and a few shook their heads.

And though no one said anything about her attire, unease grew in the pit of her stomach. Not just from the constant mention of mothers.

Why had she let Ryler talk her into coming? So, she couldn't go home for another hour. Mental note: No more scheduling workers on Saturday for her to babysit. She should have stayed on her side of the street doing just that.

But if attending the picnic would get Grayson off their backs, this torment might be worth it.

With the meal finished and cleanup done, everyone gathered at the side of the church. Under a large oak, metal chairs lined the carpet of purple, yellow, and white wildflowers.

She tugged at the hem of her shorts as she sat down. Useless. With her heels, she looked like some ridiculous bleach-blond caricature of Betty Boop. Should have worn something else. Something with a bit more coverage.

Why? She'd never been ashamed of flaunting her attributes before. But these people seemed so genuine.

Warmth rippled through her as she caught Ryler staring at her legs. It wasn't the first time. Maybe the shorts hadn't been a bad decision after all. She didn't fit in with the church people, and neither did Ryler. Two of a kind.

She caught his gaze, but he looked away.

Only a week ago, he'd invited her to dinner at Laken's. Since then, he'd been all business. Maybe they weren't two of a kind. Maybe he was above her, too. Maybe he thought her beneath him, just like everybody else did.

And wearing the shorts had only proven everyone right about her.

She needed a new image. A new wardrobe. Buttoned up, longer hemlines, and polished. She'd prove to these holier-than-thou hicks that there was more to Shell Evans than a warm bed partner.

After all, she hadn't warmed anyone's bed since Ryler had wormed his way into her heart.

Pastor Grayson cleared his throat. "Wow, look at this crowd. I'm so glad each and every one is here today. I'm especially glad to have so many visitors. If you have your Bibles, turn with me to John 8:32."

Bibles? No one had said anything about Bibles. Pages rustled as people flipped through to find the right chapter and verse.

"John 8:32, 'And ye shall know the truth, and the truth shall make you free.' Truth and freedom go together, but we only achieve freedom by putting truth into practice.

"Brothers and sisters, humble yourselves and turn to Christ. Accept His truth, that He is the living Son of God who died for our sins. Give Him the ugliness, the lies, the filthy rags of our lives. Only if we accept His truth, can we attain freedom through Him. Freedom from death and hell."

A gasp followed by a tearful cry came from the back of the crowd. "Oh my."

Shell turned to look behind her.

Six rows back, Helen Fenwick sat with a phone pressed to her ear, and tears rolling down her cheeks.

Shell hadn't noticed her at the gathering until now. But she'd surely noticed Shell and sat in the back to avoid her.

Adrea rushed to Helen's side. "What is it?"

"Wade's"—Helen's voice quivered—"dead."

four

Nausea boiled in the pit of Shell's stomach as gasps and whispers swept through the crowd.

"I always keep my phone on vibrate in case the nursing home calls. I didn't think. . ." The tearful mother's words ended on a sob and she clamped a trembling hand over quivery lips.

Grayson looked as if he might hurl. "I think we should pray." He began the prayer, pleading for strength for Helen, but the tremor in his voice proved he needed it himself.

A crushing sense of loss slumped Shell's shoulders. She stood and fled, not even stopping to check for traffic as she bolted across the highway. Her heels scuffed against gravel, but she didn't care. She stepped in a hole, and the pain of an almost sprain shot through her ankle, but she kept running.

In her apartment, she slammed the door and leaned against it. Wade. Dead.

It couldn't be. Just yesterday, Adrea had dumped him. He'd started drinking again, then convinced Shell to move to Missouri—to start over—

A knock jarred the door against her back. She jumped.

&

"Shell, you okay?" Ryler pressed his ear against the door, expecting her to ignore him. After all, he'd claimed to be all business then asked her to Laken's dinner party, and this picnic. She must be as confused about him as he was her.

"I'm fine." Her voice cracked.

He winced. "No, you're not. Let me in."

"Really, I'm fine." *Watery sounding.*

"I'm not leaving until I can see you're really okay." Ryler pounded on the aged wood again. What was he doing? Exactly what he'd advised Collin to do with Jill, if he cared.

The lock clicked.

He pushed the door open.

Pacing the living room, she didn't acknowledge him.

"I guess you knew the old guy who died?" *Duh.*

"He wasn't old." She hugged herself. "I was engaged to him once."

Ryler's gut twisted. She'd loved someone. Someone other than him. Maybe that's why she'd never been able to commit. "But I thought he was in the nursing home."

"It's a long story and one I don't want to get into right now." Tucking a silky strand behind her ear, she hurried to her bedroom. "The heat-and-air guy is almost finished and I'm going home for the weekend. Now."

"You okay to drive?"

While she dug a suitcase out from under her bed, he stood in the doorway, appreciating the scenery. *Jerk, she's upset and you're checking her out.*

She nodded, set the case on the bed, and started stuffing clothes inside. "Will you lock up after the workers leave? I'll be back late Sunday evening."

"Want me to drive you, since you're upset and all?"

"No."

Her answer came too quick, as if she were hiding something.

With a shaky hand, she raked her hair back from her face. It fell about her shoulders like a silky curtain in some shampoo commercial.

"I'm fine. But thanks for caring." She frowned, as if his caring confused her.

It did him, too.

"I'll let you be then. See you Monday." He turned to go, but a thought hit him. "Do you want to go to the funeral?"

She bit her lip and fresh tears filled her eyes.

Stop looking like that, woman. It made him want to kiss all her hurt away.

"I'm not sure yet."

"If you want to. . ." He cleared his throat. "I could go with you—I mean—just so you don't have to go alone."

"That's very sweet," she squeaked. "I'll think about it while I'm gone and let you know."

Turn toward the door. Run. Run while you still can.

"All right then. Safe trip." He hurried outside and around the big house.

Settling on the iron bench in the front garden, he could see the church lot had cleared already.

Why had he followed her? Why did he care if she cried? Why did he care if she was hiding something?

Because he still loved her. Just because she'd dumped him, his feelings hadn't died.

❧

In the JC Penney dressing room, Shell smoothed the black sheath over her flat stomach and turned sideways in the mirror. The high neck, short sleeves, and hemline barely above her knees was unlike anything she'd normally buy. But the only little black dress she owned would just solidify the further impression that Shell Evans was nothing more than a bimbo.

Not dowdy, this dress still showed her curves, but left everything else to the imagination. Perfect for the funeral. She almost looked respectable.

With satisfaction she shrugged out of it and back into her jeans and shirt. On the way to the register, she picked several cotton camisoles in different shades. The blouses she owned all had low necklines. But with something underneath, they'd be totally decent. She paid and strode out of the store feeling better about herself already.

The least she could do for Wade was show up at his funeral fully clothed.

Funeral. She shuddered.

Did she want Ryler to go with her? Did she need him to?

He hadn't reissued the offer, so maybe she'd just leave it at that.

"Why, hello, dear. Fancy meeting you in Searcy."

Sylvie Kroft.

Shell turned to face her. "Hello."

"I saw you at the picnic Saturday, but I was on kitchen duty, so I never got to even say hi to you. I'm a member at Palisade."

And that's supposed to impress me?

"Listen, Shell, you probably know me as a gossip, but I've repented of my tart tongue. I'd like to apologize for hurting you in the past. You were just a child when you came to Thorndike, and I personally ran you out on a rail. For that, I'm truly sorry."

"Don't you know who her mother is?" Sylvie's voice hissed from the past.

"Okay." Uncertainty echoed in Shell's tone.

"Really, I'm not in the gossip mill business any longer. Do you have dinner plans?"

Shell couldn't think of anything she'd rather do less. Having her legs waxed perhaps? Not even that.

"No ulterior motives, I promise. I'll even buy and you can pick the place."

Might as well get a free steak out of the deal. "How about Colton's?"

"Oh, I love that place." Sylvie clasped her jeweled hands together. "The first time I went there with a friend, I was kind of iffy. I mean peanut shells? On the floor? But I guess it grew on me and the steaks are excellent."

"I'll meet you there." Shell checked her watch. "What time?"

"Now, if you're finished shopping."

"I am."

"All right then." Sylvie beamed. "I'll see you there."

She could just drive home. Stand Sylvie up. After all, it was probably a trap. She wanted information. Probably about Wade. After spreading rumors for years, Sylvie couldn't possibly have changed that much.

"Please show up." Sylvie's tone pleaded. "I imagine you don't trust me. I've given you ample reason not to, but I'd like to make it up to you."

Like a steak could fix it all.

"I'll be there." She wasn't a child anymore. If Sylvie tried anything, she could stand up to this woman and tell her what she really thought of her. Once and for all, put Sylvie Kroft in her place. Her hands balled into fists. The way someone should have done years ago.

Traffic on East Race inched as usual and Shell caught every red light. Even though the strip mall wasn't even a mile from the restaurant, it took ten minutes to get there.

Shell steeled her backbone, ready for a fight at the slightest jab.

Waiting inside the door, Sylvie looked relieved to see her.

"Oh good. I was worried. . ." She clamped her mouth shut. "I'm glad you could join me."

Not sure if she was glad, Shell didn't say anything.

Since it was an off night, the waitress had no problem finding them a table. Peanut shells crunched under their feet as they followed. Crying-in-your-beer music played loud. With dead, stuffed animals, branding irons, and spurs decorating the walls behind her, Sylvie didn't blend into their surroundings at all. They sat across from one another in a booth with mirrors lining the wall beside them.

Sylvie patted Shell's hand. "How are you doing since Wade's death? Oh dear, I still have a lot to learn about tact, don't I? I'm not being nosy. I promise. I just know it must be hard on you. You loved him at one time."

"Or I wouldn't have stolen him from Adrea." Shell's veins boiled. "Is that what you're getting at?"

Sylvie's watermelon-tinted lips pursed. "You don't trust my motives, and I don't blame you."

The waitress came and they both ordered sweet teas.

With a shaky, bejeweled hand, Sylvie tucked her hair behind her ear. "Let me tell you something. When I was seventeen, I wasn't married and I got pregnant."

Shell's jaw dropped.

"That's right. Martin and I weren't married and I got pregnant. Back then, it was still somewhat of a scandal in well-to-do families like mine."

"So, Collin. . . ?"

"No, before Collin. My parents were horrified. They moved to Little Rock to avoid the humiliation and forced me to give my son up for adoption."

Shell's heart twisted. "You don't even know where he is?"

Shaking her head, tears filled Sylvie's eyes. "For years, I was so ashamed and tried to make sure no one found out. I latched on to any rumor I could find and spread it like wildfire. I guess I thought if I kept enough gossip circulating, no one would find out about my secret."

"I'm sorry." Shell swallowed. At least she knew where Chance was. "No mother should have to give up a child."

"No." Sylvie's voice was barely a whisper. "We're trying to find him now, but we haven't had much luck. So, now with my bombshell, maybe you might trust me. Are you okay? Do you plan to go to the funeral?"

"I came to Searcy to buy a new dress for it." Her voice quivered.

"I think you should go. Funerals are for the living. If you don't go, you might never have closure. What about the visitation? I think it's tonight."

"No. I thought it might be too hard on the family for me to show up."

Sylvie patted her hand. "You should go if you want to. Adrea is over what happened and I imagine Helen is by now. They're both very forgiving souls. You can trust me on that. I've hurt them both. They should never give me the time of day, but you'd think nothing ever happened."

Visitation? Standing around looking at Wade? Dead Wade. No way.

"Do you really think they're over the past? Or just covering how they really feel?"

"Adrea and Helen aren't the type who can cover their feelings, and I honestly don't think they could harbor ill will toward anyone. For very long, anyway. We should all be more like them." Sylvie laughed. "I never would have dreamed I'd say such a thing."

The waitress brought their teas and took their order.

When she'd agreed to the meal, Shell had planned to order the most expensive item on the menu just to stick it to Sylvie. But now she ordered what she actually wanted. Sirloin tips. She could almost taste the savory meat, onions, and peppers. Baked sweet potato with sugar, cinnamon, and butter. Yum. Why didn't all restaurants offer it instead of the traditional potato?

She waited until the waitress left. "So, why the change in you?"

"For a long time, God's been poking me in the ribs every time I cause people problems. And for a long time I ignored Him." Sylvie's chin trembled. "I guess it got to where the pokes were so frequent, my ribs bruised. And I wanted everyone to pray for me to find my son. Why would anyone want to pray for me if all I did was cause them pain?"

Sylvie sucked in a quivery breath. "That part sounds selfish, but I long for him so. Sometimes, my arms literally ache from wanting to give him a hug."

Shell's throat convulsed as she tried to swallow the large lump there. "I'd like to make a new start. I'm tired of everyone hating me and looking down on me."

"I don't know anyone who hates you or looks down on you. It could be your imagination." Sylvie sipped her tea.

"You, of all people, know what my reputation is. I didn't even have anything decent to wear to the funeral." *All my clothes have plunging necklines and thigh-high hems.*

"Did you find something?"

"I did. It's nothing like I've ever owned. I think Wade's death made me realize life is short. Just because my mother is a certain way and raised me a certain way, I don't have to follow in her footsteps."

Up until now, her life was like that old country-and-western song "Looking for Love in All the Wrong Places." If there was love out there waiting, she wanted to find it in the right place. Maybe with Ryler. Could he return her love?

If she could reinvent herself, could she be Chance's mother?

"If you don't mind me asking, how is your mother, dear?"

"She got out of jail a few months ago." *Solicitation.* Such an innocent-sounding word. Her gaze lowered to the table. *At least I never did that.* "I think she's back in on drug charges."

"You poor dear. I'm sorry. Truly I am." Sylvie patted her hand. "You know, speaking of a new image, I've been thinking about getting a makeover. Maybe a softer look would warm up my image. Red isn't my natural color. My hair is actually brown with auburn highlights like Laken's."

"So, you're going natural."

"Actually, I've been thinking I might go a soft blond." Sylvie scanned her appearance in the mirror beside them. "According to my hairdresser, as we age, our skin fades and our hair along with it. So maybe a light shade would make me seem kinder, gentler, less of a busybody."

"Mine's mousy brown, but I've been thinking of going with more of a slightly darker shade." *Less bleach-blond bimbo.*

"If you're sure about not going to visitation, I'll call my hairdresser and see if she can get us in this evening."

"Now?"

"I tip well enough, so she usually drops everything to get me in. I'll buy. Operation makeover, change our image, here we come." Sylvie offered her hand.

With a smile, Shell shook it, just as the waitress brought their food.

&

Mid-spring called for no pantyhose. Some man who'd never had to wriggle into them had surely invented the things.

As Shell pulled the dress up over her shoulders, a knock sounded at her front door. "Just a minute."

She tugged the dress in place and hurried to the door, zipping as she went. "Who is it?"

"Ryler."

Smoothing her hands over her hair, she slipped peep-toe heels on, clasped her fake pearl necklace, and opened the door.

"Hey." His eyes widened. "You look. . .great."

"Thanks." She took in his appearance. Tan Dockers and a

seafoam green polo. His eyes blended with the shirt. "You're mighty spiffy yourself. Going somewhere?"

"To the funeral. That is—if you need me to."

Shell swallowed to dislodge the knot in her throat.

"I know we didn't say anything else about it. But I thought I'd come prepared. No pressure." Ryler held his hands up, palms toward her. "I stashed work clothes in the truck."

Not walking in alone would be nice. "I'd appreciate it if you'd go with me. A lot."

"Walk or drive? The parking lot's filling up, but those shoes look painful. Nice, but painful." He grinned.

"They're really not bad." She peered around him but couldn't see past the big house. "Let's walk. I don't plan on going to the cemetery." There was only so much she could take.

He offered his arm. "Did you do something different with your hair?"

She tucked her fingers in his elbow and they headed down the gravel drive. "It was weird. I went to Searcy last night to buy this dress and I ran into Sylvie Kroft."

Ryler cleared his throat. "I did some work for her once."

"I knew her when I was a kid. She was the meanest, most hateful woman. She delighted in unearthing skeletons from people's pasts or families and telling everyone all about it. I couldn't stand her." A piece of gravel turned under her heel and she clutched Ryler's rock-hard bicep.

"But last night, she was like a different person. She apologized for hurting me in the past and told me her life story with a few secrets of her own."

"What kind of secrets?"

"A lady doesn't tell another lady's secrets, now does she?" She lifted an eyebrow. But she wasn't a lady, no matter how conservatively she dressed. "She's changed and is really quite nice. We shared a very enjoyable dinner and then went and got a makeover. We both decided we needed a new image."

"Sounds like an eventful evening." He covered her hand with his. "You really look great—I mean—you did before, too, but now your hair's more. . ."

"Natural? The hairdresser put darker streaks in so it would look highlighted instead of bleached." Her words probably sounded like Greek to him, but his compliments made her nervous. His biceps made her nervous. His presence made her nervous.

"Whatever. It looks real. . .nice."

As they neared the highway, pleasant small talk could no longer distract her from their destination. She sucked in a shuddery breath. "I wish I didn't have to do this."

"Nobody said you had to. We can turn around and march right back to your apartment."

"I need to do it."

"The lady's wish is my command."

Lady. That word again. As if they were both playing a game.

They stopped at the highway and checked for traffic then strode across.

"Oh, Shell, there you are." A newly soft-blond Sylvie stepped from her car.

Ryler stiffened.

"I brought something for you." Sylvie handed her a large velvet box. "I thought these would set off your dress, so I decided to let you borrow them for today. I see you thought the same thing."

"You really shouldn't have." Shell flipped the lid open to find a strand of pearls. For a moment, she couldn't find her tongue. Her hand went to the costume strand she wore. "Are they real?"

"They're cultured, which isn't the ultra-pricey, rare kind, but yes, they're real. Our family has a tradition. My grandmother and mother each had pearls and they passed them down to me. These are mine. They'll go to my youngest, Laken, someday. My mother's necklace will go to Collin." Sylvie's chin trembled. "My grandmother's strand went to our oldest son."

Ryler cleared his throat. "We better get inside, ladies. Or we won't be able to find a seat."

"Here, Ryler. You do the honors." Sylvie gently scooped the pearls from the box and handed them to him.

With shaky hands, he accepted.

Why was he nervous? Was it the value of the pearls? Or did Sylvie rattle him?

"I really couldn't borrow your family heirloom." Shell shook her head.

"Yes, you can. I insist. Now, hold your hair out of the way, dear."

Shell did as instructed, removed her necklace, and turned her back toward Ryler.

His breath fanned the back of her neck and she shivered. Eternity passed as he fumbled with the catch. Finally, it fastened into place.

"Perfect." Sylvie clasped her hands together. "Now, take a deep breath. My grandmother used to say, 'Nothing's as bad as you think it'll be except for funerals, but they don't last long.'"

Ryler's jaw clenched. "Listen, Shell, with Mrs. Kroft here, you've got all the support you need. I'll just go."

"No." She grabbed his arm.

"I'll leave y'all alone." Sylvie stashed the necklace box in her car and went inside.

"I can't tell you how much I appreciate you coming with me." Tears stung Shell's eyes. "I'd really like you to stay."

He tucked her fingers in his elbow.

Side by side, they entered the church. Shell hadn't been in one since she was nine.

Burgundy carpet with matching padded pews. A huge harp sat on one side of the stage with a piano on the other. Prisms of light bounced off the stained glass windows.

The coffin sat in front of the pulpit with part of the lid open. Shell averted her eyes from the waxy figure inside. Her stomach clenched as an usher tried to direct them to the front.

"Please, I'd rather sit toward the back."

Ryler nodded and ignored the usher.

Three pews from the back. Far enough that she couldn't see inside the coffin. Maybe she could do this.

"I've never been to a funeral," she whispered.

"Never?" His eyebrow lifted. "I've only been to one."

"Whose was it?"

He swallowed. "My parents'."

"Both of them? How old were you?"

"Eighteen. House fire."

"I'm so sorry." She threaded her fingers into his and squeezed his hand.

"Me, too."

Haunting organ music played as the church filled to capacity. Wade had not been this popular. What was the deal?

Two men in dark suits strode to the front of the church. One moved the flowers from the casket, while the other tucked in satin fabric and shut the lid.

Shell flinched.

Wade was in the box—with the lid closed.

Ryler squeezed her hand.

With solemn dignity, Grayson escorted Helen, her sister June, and Adrea to the front pew. Mark and Grace joined them there as Helen dabbed her eyes. Once everyone was seated, Grayson climbed the few steps to the stage and sat in one of the large wooden chairs facing the congregation.

Soon the music faded away and Grayson stood. "I'd like to thank everyone for coming today. What a great show of love and support for Helen. She'll need each and every one of you over the next several months. Let us pray."

Shell tuned out. So, these people weren't here for Wade, but for his mother.

"Amen." Grayson read the obituary, insignificant details of Wade's life, and his family, which wasn't much to speak of. Most had preceded him in death. "The thing about death is we never know when it's coming. When Wade woke up Saturday morning, he didn't know it would be the last time he awoke in this life."

He didn't know anything. The last time Shell had seen

him, he'd been in a hospital bed, curled to one side, with drool running down one side of his mouth.

"Thankfully, Wade had accepted salvation years ago and shortly before his injury, he rededicated his life to Christ. And we know that God is just."

What? When did that happen? In between bars? In between women? In between rehab stints? While he'd been engaged to Adrea and sleeping with Shell? Why was Grayson sugarcoating Wade's life? How could he stand over the coffin of the man who'd killed his wife and act like Wade was a saint?

"I promised Helen I'd share a simple plan of salvation. If anyone here doesn't know Jesus as their personal Savior, make that decision today and leave here with the assurance of heaven."

Shell's heart pounded in her ears. Pressure welled in her chest. She'd felt this way before in church. When she was a kid. She concentrated on the burgundy fabric lining the back of the pew in front of her.

"Pray this prayer with me: Dear Jesus, I know I'm a sinner. Thank You for dying on the cross for my sins. Please forgive me. I'm making a new start. I trust You completely and accept You as my Lord and Savior, Jesus. Amen.

"Folks, with that simple prayer, you can make a difference in where you spend eternity. Heaven or hell? You must make a choice. If you don't make a decision, then the decision is already made for you. Where will you spend eternity?"

The words echoed in Shell's ears. As the service ended, she could hardly breathe. The pianist started playing and the ushers reopened the casket then stepped toward the aisle. The people in the pew just behind Helen stood, then one by one, they walked to the casket.

Shell jabbed Ryler in the ribs. "What are they doing?"

"It's customary."

A few people paused at the casket, while others barely glanced.

"I can't," she whispered then jumped up and ran to the lobby. Standing room only, she wove her way through the crowd and out the doors.

Fresh air filled her lungs and her breathing eased. As fast as her heels would carry her, she scurried across the road and straight to her apartment.

A few of the workers called out greetings, but she didn't respond.

Inside, she sank into the couch, covering her face with her hands.

"Where will you spend eternity?"

Could Wade really go to heaven after all the things he'd done? After all the people he'd hurt? After killing Sara Sterling? After attempting to kill himself?

❧

Ryler's fist hovered at the frame of Shell's door. *Haven't we played this scene before?* For the second time, she'd fled from the church and ran blindly home. Both times, he'd followed. Why?

He knocked. "It's Ryler. You okay?"

"I'm fine."

"You don't sound fine."

"That's because I'm not." She opened the door.

Tears shimmering on her cheeks tore at his insides. "You loved him?"

"I didn't know how to love then." Hugging herself, she paced the small living room. "I just can't believe he's dead."

"I heard it was pneumonia."

She shivered. "But he'd been dying for two years."

"Something about an attempted suicide."

She whirled to face him. "How did you know that?"

"I heard somebody say something at the gas station the other day."

"I bet they all blamed it on me."

Ryler frowned. "How could you have had anything to do with it?"

Her chin dropped to her chest. Her shoulders shook and a sob escaped.

Why did she always have to cry around him? It was like she knew he couldn't take it.

He pulled her into his arms, her sobs shaking them both. As he stroked her hair, she soaked his shoulder. The sobs eased and she trembled against him.

So soft, so beautiful, and her perfume could drive a man insane. He buried his face in her hair, grazing his lips across her ear.

She pulled away enough to gaze up at him, her full lips begging.

As if drawn by an irresistible magnetic pull, he lowered his mouth toward hers.

She stood on tiptoe.

five

Heat swirled through Ryler's veins as their lips met. As if the last six months apart had never happened. Striving for control, he traced kisses over her jaw.

"Let's move this party to my bedroom," Shell whispered, deep and throaty.

He pulled away to look into her eyes. The tears were gone, but the damage to her makeup remained. Inside and out. Her lips trembled with vulnerability.

He took a step backward. "You're upset."

"So?" She shrugged. "Make me feel better."

"I've done a lot of horrible things in my life, but I've never taken advantage of a woman."

She stepped close to him. "It's not taking advantage when I'm willing. Quite willing." Her smile promised pleasure.

Closing his eyes, he took another step backward. "You're not thinking straight and I'm leaving. Now."

"Jerk. You're just like all the rest."

He winced. "I used to be. If I still was, I'd be in your bed by now. Then I'd sneak out after you fell asleep." But he was trying to be a better man. The kind of man his parents raised him to be. "I want to stay. Believe me, with everything in me, I want to stay."

"So, stay."

"I can't. You're in no shape to know what you want. Or don't want." He took another step toward the door. "But you shouldn't be alone. Pull yourself together and meet me in the office. We'll talk."

"Talk?" She propped a hand on her hip.

Why, oh why, did nobility have to hit him now? He'd never done a noble thing in his adult life. She'd offered herself and he was leaving. Offering to talk instead.

But he didn't want to be just another regret on her long list. And he didn't want to hurt her. She'd obviously been hurt enough.

"I'll be in the office. Come on up when you're ready." He winked and hurried out the door.

Regret tugged at him. Oh, how badly he wanted to turn around and give in to her.

But for the first time in years, he knew he'd done the right thing. His parents would be proud. Knowing that put a warm bubble in his chest.

Still. Maybe a cold shower. . .

≫

Shell pressed her fist against quivery lips. Why had Ryler left? He'd never turned her down. No man ever had.

Rejection weighed heavily on her shoulders. Yet, it was weird. He hadn't wanted to leave. It wasn't that he didn't find her desirable. It was almost like he'd left because he—cared.

The last thing she wanted was to talk, but she couldn't let him know his rejection bothered her. She had to pull herself together fast.

She doused her face with cold water and changed into her jeans. Her white plunging V-neck transformed into decent with the new aqua camisole underneath. Though she managed to get rid of the tear streaks with fresh foundation and blush, the red-rimmed puffiness around her eyes refused to go away.

But Ryler already knew she'd been crying and the crew knew she'd been to a funeral, so she had a good excuse.

She slid her feet into white sandals, closed the door behind her, and hurried to the big house. Power tools hummed on the other side now. Unseen, she entered through the back door, darted to the front entry, and climbed the stairs.

"There you are." Ryler swayed slowly on the porch swing and patted the seat beside him. With one finger, he drew an imaginary line down the center. "No crossing this line. We're just talking."

She grinned. No matter what the situation, his humor

always eased her worries. One of the many, many, many things she liked about him. She perched at the far end of the swing.

"Feel any better?"

"Not really. Tell me about your parents—I mean—if it doesn't bother you."

"They were great. I was the center of their universe. We went to church every time the doors were open. They spent every spare minute coddling me and each other." He frowned. "But we had a falling-out just after my eighteenth birthday and I left."

"For how long?"

"Three days after I left, they died."

Shell gasped.

"It was the stupid Christmas tree lights. They never woke up."

She closed her eyes. "I'm really sorry."

"Our argument seems so insignificant now." He ran a hand through his hair, sending waves tumbling. "But then, I was young and hotheaded. I felt like my entire life was a lie and I could never forgive them for it."

Hindsight. She knew all about it. And now guilt ate at him.

"All those hours I spent angry with them. Wasted. They were just trying to protect me. If only I'd been there."

"It's not your fault." Her fingers itched to touch his arm.

"I'm a light sleeper, so I probably would have woken up."

"Or you might have died with them." A cold chill crept down Shell's spine.

"I think I could have lived with that better." A smile tugged at his mouth. "You know what I mean."

I couldn't have lived without you better. "It must have been really rough."

A sparrow perched on the rail under the feeder but noticed them and swooped away.

Ryler nodded. "I made it. How about you?"

Shell huffed out a big breath. "I never knew my father." She wasn't sure if her mom even knew who he was.

"I'm sorry."

"It's no big deal." Her voice broke. With a wince, she

shrugged. "I have an older sister, Savannah." *She doesn't know who her father is either.* But they were probably two different men since the sisters didn't favor one another at all. "Mom was originally from Savannah and loved the beach, so that's how she chose our names. It isn't Michelle or Shelly, just Shell."

"A unique name for a unique lady."

There was that word again. She wanted to roll her eyes, especially after what had happened back at her apartment between them.

"It must have been nice having a sibling."

"Painful, too." Her teeth sank into her bottom lip.

"You didn't get along?"

"We were extremely close." So close that when one of them went through something bad, the other ached, too. And there was a lot of bad stuff. Her mind transported to the distant memory. "When I was ten, Mom's boyfriend raped Savannah. She was twelve and he was coming after me next, but Mom got home in time to stop him."

Ryler's sharp intake of breath shook her back to the present.

"I didn't mean to tell you that. It just sort of popped out. I've never told anyone."

"Did the pervert go to jail?"

Closing her eyes, she nodded. "DHS almost took us away. But my sister and I didn't want to be separated, so we lied about how stable Mom was and what good care she took of us."

After that, she seemed to pay more attention to them. "Savannah was in therapy for years, but she's happily married now and raising my"—panic clamped Shell's mouth closed—"my nephew, with another on the way."

Gleeful laughter echoed from next door.

His hands balled into fists. "Did any of your mom's other boyfriends ever try anything?"

"When I was seventeen, but I hit him in the head with a beer bottle and jabbed the broken neck of it at him until he left." He didn't come back and Mom blamed Shell.

Ryler touched her hand.

"You crossed the line." She grinned.

"No child should be raised like that." Ryler swallowed hard.

"I left after that. Savannah had just gotten married and I lived with her and her husband for about a year and finished high school."

"Did you ever see your mom again?"

"No, but she calls Savannah every time she lands in jail." Shell picked at a hangnail and flinched when it got into the quick. "All her years of hard living took a toll on her looks, so she turned to other means of making her living. She's been arrested for solicitation numerous times and lately drugs. *Solicitation.* Isn't that a harmless-sounding word? I can't say that I've been a saint, but I never did that and I've never drank or done drugs."

Ryler squeezed her hand. "You learned too young that most men only want sex, and you confused that with love. I haven't been a saint either, but I only loved once. And too late, I realized she didn't love me."

Could he be talking about her? Or someone else? Her lips twitched and she pressed her hand to her mouth.

"Sex doesn't equal love, Shell. Don't let anybody tell you it does. I'm sorry if I ever made you feel used."

No. That last bit about making her feel used proved he'd never loved her. If only he could.

"I'm hot." She pressed her wrist against the sweat beading her brow. "I mean—it's hot out here."

"If you don't mind me rifling through your house, I'll get you a glass of tea."

"Sounds great."

"Then we'll talk about Darrell's latest idea about the front waterfall." He disappeared through the door.

Why had she told him all that? What a day. Her first funeral. Her first rejection. Her first confession.

Maybe it was the calming balcony. His soothing presence. The *whir* of power tools assuring no one would overhear the conversation.

Or maybe loving him brought out her vulnerable side.

At least she hadn't confessed everything.

❧

Ryler stared at the white foam of water cascading down the jutting rocks into the blue-green pool below.

Beside him, standing on a natural balcony, where numerous couples had recited their wedding vows, Shell gazed out over the falls. "Isn't it beautiful?"

Not as beautiful as she was. The only woman he'd ever loved, and he'd almost told her the truth two days ago.

A slight breeze blew her hair in a silken tumble. Red nails peeped at him from matching high-heeled sandals. Her jeans had a hole in the knee, giving him a tantalizing glimpse of her leg now and then. Her red top, edged with white lace, set off her tanned skin. One delicate hand gripped the railing. If he moved his fingers over a couple of inches, he could touch her.

Emotions tumbled within him as violently as the gush of water over the falls.

Concentrate.

"Darrell wants the Romance Waterfalls in the front yard of the B & B?"

"On a much smaller scale, of course. I thought it might help if you saw the real thing."

He couldn't care less about the falls. All he cared about was the woman standing so close to him. He wanted the chance to kiss her again. To show her what a real kiss could be. He'd blown it the other day.

Next time, it would be less about passion. More about love and respect. Like he'd never kissed anyone. Despite their past intimacies, with her, it hadn't been all sex. At least not for him.

Her laugh made him dizzy. Her fighting spirit made him want to fight for her. Her strength made him feel invincible.

He wanted more from her. A lifetime?

"It'll take months and make this job last forever."

"I've got time." He swatted at a persistent gnat.

Time to win her heart.

"Yeah, well, I don't. All I want is to finish this job and go home."

"I'll work as quickly as I can. You'll be here another six weeks anyway, working on the interior."

How had she woven her silken web around his heart so completely? So quickly? Her wounded soul cried out to him. Begging for a healing love. And for the first time, he felt he had it to give. And for the first time, he was certain, if he could win her love, she'd never abandon him.

She needed a real love as much as he did. If only he could fill the hole in her heart. He'd lost her once, and couldn't stand to think of losing her again.

"Hello?" She punched his shoulder.

"Hmm."

"What do you think?"

"About what?"

"About how long will this take?"

How could she be so unaffected, when he could barely breathe with her so near? Because she didn't feel the same way. What was he thinking? She'd already abandoned him once.

He cleared his throat. "I'll take plenty of pictures and see what I can come up with. An extra month or so should complete the whole project."

A regret-filled sigh escaped her.

Obviously, she was looking forward to him wrapping up and leaving her alone.

She turned away from the railing. "What are those droopy lavender flowers on the fence where we first came in?"

"Wisteria. It's a vine."

"I think we need some at the B & B."

"I'll see what I can do. They don't bloom very long, but they're very fragrant."

"And pretty. Let's walk down to the bottom, so we can get the full scope of the waterfall."

As she started down the natural stone steps, he grabbed her hand. "Watch your step." Electricity shot up his arm. Any excuse just to touch her again. However fleeting their time together might be.

❧

Shell clutched the chain of the swing with one hand and leaned forward to peer through the newly installed balcony railing. The last day of a long workweek.

Playing in the dirt as usual, Ryler whistled a happy tune while spreading black plastic sheeting where the falls would go in the front yard. A pile of large natural rocks waited.

The terra-cotta scalloped edging and matching stepping-stones led to the fountain, surrounded by numerous rosebushes and plants. Pink, red, yellow, orange, and purple wilted blossoms soaked up the sunlight, struggling with their new home. But Ryler promised he could coax them to life.

Closing her eyes, she leaned her temple against the hand clutching the chain. Try as she might, she couldn't forget the heat of his kiss, the feel of his arms around her, the respect he'd treated her with.

She just wanted to go home.

To Chance.

Away from Ryler.

Oh, for this job to end, this constant contact with him to be over, these odd feelings he stirred within her to stop.

But instead their time together had been extended.

Power tools created a constant *buzz* and *whir* in the background. Shell heard the noise in her sleep. There was something relaxing about the sound.

"If you're asleep, I hate to wake you."

Shell jumped.

Sylvie Kroft stood in the doorway of the landing. "I'm sorry. I hated to let you get a crick in your neck."

"I wasn't asleep. Just thinking." Shell reached under her hair to unfasten the pearls. "I forgot to give you these. I've been a nervous wreck about them and decided the safest place for them was around my neck. I wasn't trying to keep them."

"I know that, dear, and that's not why I came." Sylvie took

the necklace, tucked it in her handbag, and sat next to Shell. "I saw how upset you were when you left the funeral the other day, and I haven't seen you since. So, I thought I should check on you."

"I've never attended a funeral before. I didn't know you were supposed to walk by the casket." Her voice cracked. "I couldn't do it."

"Barbaric practice if you ask me." Sylvie's nose scrunched. "So hard on the family. And in my busybody days, I used to go to funerals just to see how good or bad people looked. I told Martin to close my casket and seal it shut whenever it's my turn."

Shell shivered. *Where will you spend eternity?*

The power tools stopped in unison. Quitting time.

A child's giggle echoed in the sudden silence.

Another shiver sent goose bumps over Shell.

"That must be tough. Listening to the tinkling laughter of a child on a daily basis."

Shell frowned. Could Sylvie know?

"I know your baby died and I'm truly sorry. Though my son lived, I know what it feels like to lose a child."

Tears singed Shell's eyes. "How did you know?" Or think she knew.

"I never told anyone about your loss." Sylvie patted her arm. "That's not gossip fodder, even for a former gossip-maven like me. I assume it was a miscarriage, but you should be able to have other children. What did the doctor say?"

"I think that's enough." Ryler's steely voice came from the doorway.

"I'm not trying to stir up any trouble." Sylvie jumped up. "Since I was once forced to give up a child, I thought I could help Shell."

"It's not helping and it's time for you to go. Shell's had enough drama lately."

Shell wiped a tear. "She didn't mean anything, Ryler. Sylvie's been very kind to me."

"It's okay. I should go. Truly, I only want to help." Sylvie patted Shell's arm and turned toward the house.

"I just bet you do," Ryler snarled at the retreating woman's back.

"What was that about?"

"I've heard all about her. She's not being nice. She's digging for ammo to use against you."

"I don't think so. I honestly think she wanted to help. Did you know she has another son and she doesn't even know where he is? Her parents made her give him up."

Ryler ran a hand through his hair. "That's her take on it."

"I've seen the pain in her eyes. Her arms ache to hug him." Shell hugged herself. She knew the ache Sylvie spoke of. "She thought our experiences were similar enough that we might mourn together."

"We're clearing out," the foreman called from beneath the balcony. "See ya in the morning."

"Thanks." Ryler waved.

He turned back toward her. "I'm sorry about your baby. I didn't know."

Shell tried to hold back the tears, but they rimmed her lashes. She'd already had one meltdown in front of him in the short time he'd been back in her life. She blinked several times, but her vision didn't clear.

As the last of the convoy of work trucks pulled out of the drive, Ryler sat beside her and pulled her into his arms once more.

In his arms, she could no longer hold it together. Her shoulders shook and sobs knifed through her. She wanted to tell him everything, but what would he think of her?

Pulling away from him, she stood, and walked toward the railing. "He's alive."

"What?"

Wiping her tears with the back of her hand, she turned to face him. "My son didn't die."

Ryler's gaze narrowed. "Where is he? Why does Sylvie think he died?"

"It's a long story."

"I've got time."

Might as well tell him all of it. She stared down the long drive toward the church. "When I first met Wade, he was engaged to Adrea. He was an alcoholic but had been sober for two years."

"They broke up and you helped him pick up the pieces?"

"I wish." She shook her head, disgusted. "I broke them up. She came to see him and I was supposed to hide in his bedroom, but I made sure she saw me."

He frowned, disappointment written all over his face.

But he loved her. Not me. And he couldn't get over her. "They were supposed to get married on Valentine's Day. Instead"— she trembled—"he went on a binge, ran a red light, and had a head-on collision."

"Was anyone hurt?"

"Grayson Sterling and his first wife, Sara, were in the other car. She died."

Ryler winced.

"Wade left the scene, didn't tell a soul he was responsible, and asked me to move with him to his aunt's in Missouri."

"Did he tell you what happened?"

"Not at first. He ran to Missouri supposedly so we could start over. A few years later, I found out I was pregnant. I guess he wanted a clean slate, so he confessed." *Which freaked me out.* "I left, but he followed me back here. At that point, I just wanted him out of my life, so I told him I'd aborted the baby."

Ryler's jaw clenched. "But you didn't."

"I planned to, but I couldn't do it."

"I'm glad." He squeezed her hand.

"Me, too." She closed her eyes. "Anyway, Wade made a confession at the church, then shot himself in the head. He's been in a vegetative state in the nursing home ever since."

"And your son?"

"My sister's raising him."

"You gave him away?" Dropping her hand, Ryler backed away from her. His accusing green eyes sliced through her.

She cowered under his gaze. She'd been wrong about him.

She'd thought he was different, but he was just like everyone else in this judgmental town.

Shaking his head, Ryler whirled around and stalked to the door. He slammed it behind him so hard she thought surely the glass would break. It didn't.

But her heart did.

❧

Ryler flicked his turn signal on, needing a sane presence. No cars sat in the post office lot. He parked and killed the engine.

Half a day lost, dealing with Shell. And she was just like his mother. She'd thrown her son away. An inconvenience. At least she'd let him live.

How could he have been such a fool? He'd sworn off women. Vowed he'd never let anyone near his heart ever again. But Shell had crooked her finger and he'd fallen over himself to get close to her all over again.

He should have known he couldn't trust her when she'd so easily taken up with Sylvie. Two of a kind. He opened the truck door and climbed out.

Laken was the only sane one in the family. How had she turned out okay?

A blast of humid air propelled him inside. He inserted the key into his mailbox and pulled out a handful of bills then continued to the clerk station.

"Hey. How are you today?" Her bright smile couldn't calm the storm in his soul.

"Okay."

She tapped her chin with her fingernail. "You don't seem okay."

"How's Collin? Did he and Jill work things out? I haven't managed to catch him home lately."

"They're fine. He said you gave him advice that worked."

"Good. She seemed like a nice lady." He shuffled the mail in his hand. "Can I ask you a question that's really none of my business?"

"You can ask. I may not answer."

"Why does Brady live with you and Hayden?"

Laken nibbled on the inside of her lip. "After his sister's death, Hayden became Brady's guardian. Collin didn't know Brady existed until last year. He blew into town intent on moving Brady to California with him. Collin's always been a bit on the selfish side." She raised her hands up, palms toward him. "But I didn't say that."

Ryler grinned. "I didn't hear a thing."

A relieved smile tugged at her mouth. "He's changed, though. God's changing him, and he finally realized how unhappy Brady was with the idea and relented."

"So why doesn't he live with Collin now?"

"Collin usually doesn't get home from work until seven each evening, while Hayden and I are home shortly after five." She tapped the countertop with a fingernail. "This is weird. I'm spilling my guts and I hardly know you. Yet, somehow I feel comfortable with you."

"I'm glad." He could barely push the words through his constricted throat, as the truth lurked on the tip of his tongue.

"Might as well keep spilling. Hayden and I are talking about me quitting work when the baby comes." A blush crept into her cheeks as she patted her stomach. "We just found out. You're the first person to know outside of family and close friends."

His throat swelled even more. Outside of family. His little sister was pregnant. "Now see, that's what parents are supposed to do. They're supposed to do what's best for their child. Not give them to someone else to raise."

She frowned. "You think Collin should work less and Brady should live with him?"

"I was thinking of someone else, not your situation. But I just don't understand why anyone would give up their child. It's not supposed to be that way." He jabbed his finger at the air. "Parents are supposed to put their kids first."

"Sometimes putting the child first means giving them up. And sometimes the parent isn't given an option."

The door opened and a woman Ryler didn't know came in.

"I better get going." He turned toward the lobby.

"Don't forget your mail," she called.

"Oh right." He nabbed the envelopes he'd left on her counter. "And, Laken, thanks for being here."

She frowned then raised one eyebrow. "You're welcome. I guess."

⋇

Shell's heart revved as she turned into the familiar drive. Home for the weekend.

Chance appeared at the window, a huge grin erupting on his face as he bounced up and down.

Her feet wouldn't move fast enough and she sprinted to the neat, brick house.

Savannah opened the kitchen door.

"Annie! Annie!" Chance cried.

He launched himself into her arms, and her vision blurred. She lifted him high in the air, twirling, and he giggled his musical laughter. Oh, to have him call her Mommy instead of Auntie.

He snuggled close, wrapping his plump arms around her neck. "Missed you."

"I missed you, too, Chance. I think I heard something about a new back tooth?"

Chance pulled away and opened wide but stuck his finger in to show her and blocked everything from view.

She laughed and dropped a kiss on his plump cheek.

"Hello, Shell." Savannah leaned against the counter, grinning at the reunion, her six-month pregnancy pooching. "We didn't expect you until tomorrow."

"I couldn't stay away from this munchkin. Not for one more minute." She traced her fingers across the bottom of Chance's bare foot sending him into giggle spasms.

"Chance, go get your new tractor to show Auntie."

Shell set him down and he vaulted toward his room as fast as his chunky legs would carry him.

"You okay?" Savannah frowned.

"I just missed him."

"What happened? Something with Ryler?"

"I told him about Chance."

Savannah's brows rose. "And."

"He walked out, disgusted that I gave Chance away."

"He doesn't understand." Savannah rested one hand on her stomach and propped the other on her hip. "You know, Jake and I were talking last night. We thought being Chance's guardians would be a short-term thing. He's your son. Not ours. We love him and we'd miss him, but we'd never fight you for custody."

Shell's eyes narrowed. "You don't want him now that you're pregnant?"

"You know that's not true." Savannah's eyes glistened.

"I'm sorry." Shell sank into an oak chair. "I shouldn't have said that."

"We love Chance. We have since the day he was born, but he's your son."

"I know and you've been there for him when I haven't." She covered her face with both hands.

A chair scraped against the tile floor and the table wobbled as Savannah sat across from her. "It's a very delicate balance, loving him, raising him, but always wondering if you'll come back and reclaim him."

And she shouldn't have put them in that position. She shouldn't have left Chance hanging in the balance.

"He's getting older. Understanding more. If you're going to reclaim him, it needs to be soon. The older he is, the harder the transition and the more confused he'll be."

"I need to get this job finished." Straightening her spine, Shell pushed the hair away from her face. "I'm thinking about asking Darrell to find someone else to finish the bed-and-breakfast. I should be here with Chance. Then things can get back to normal."

But her heart would never be normal again.

Savannah reached across the table, covering Shell's hand with her own.

Ryler climbed out of his truck and waved at Collin across the street. "Hey, neighbor."

"Got a minute?"

"Sure." Crickets and bullfrogs created a symphony in the cooling evening air.

Collin jogged across. "Jill and I went for a walk after evening church service tonight. She agreed to marry me."

"Congratulations."

"Thanks. She's a Christian, she loves me, and she's crazy about Brady."

"Sounds great."

"Except for one thing." Collin settled on the porch step.

"What's that?"

"She wants to quit working, legally adopt Brady, and have him live with us."

Why couldn't the people surrounding him raise their own kids? "And you don't want that?"

"It's exactly what I want." Collin sighed. "But number one, I want to make sure it's what Brady wants. And numbers two and three, Hayden and Laken are very attached to him. Especially Hayden. And number four, Brady is very attached to them."

"If he lives with you, he'll probably spend the weekends with Hayden and Laken." Ryler shrugged. "He'll still be close. It's not like you're taking him out of state or anything. How does Brady feel about it?"

Collin frowned, as if he wondered if Ryler knew about California. "I think he'll be fine. He and Jill get along great. And a child should be with his parents."

"I'll have to agree. In your case, your girlfriend kept you in the dark about Brady." Ryler couldn't hide the bitterness in his tone. "The people who make me sick are the ones who give up their kids because it's an inconvenience to keep them."

Collin raised one brow. "You're very passionate on the subject. Ever thought of adopting?"

"I think a child should have a mother and father figure and

I'm not interested in providing the mother figure."

"Alrighty then. Don't guess you'll want to come to my wedding."

"Actually, I'd be glad to. Just don't ask me to make it a double." Ryler smiled, hoping to take the edge off his steely tone.

"We're putting off the wedding until next year. Maybe you'll meet the perfect woman who'll change your mind by then."

Actually, he'd already met her. Or he thought he had. Had he? "Don't hold your breath. Why wait so long?"

"Beats me. I'd get hitched tomorrow." Collin rolled his eyes. "But she wants to do the whole Valentine's thing in Romance."

"How cheesy can you get?" Ryler chuckled.

Collin frowned.

"Sorry." Ryler's grin flattened and he clapped Collin on the back. "I'll back you up, bro." His eyes widened. Tiny slip. Called his brother, bro. No reaction from Collin.

Ryler blew out a big breath. That was close.

❧

Clutching the doorknob, Shell closed her eyes. Monday morning. Her first encounter with Ryler since she'd told him the truth.

Just do it. Open the door. Face him. Work with the carpenters. Get this place finished and go home. It's in the home stretch. Five more weeks. She couldn't bow out on Darrell with only five weeks left to completion.

The plumber was finished. The new bathrooms had walls. Now it was up to the woodworking guys.

She turned the knob.

On his hands and knees beside the back fountain, Ryler looked up then quickly averted his gaze.

Willing herself not to run, she nonchalantly strode to the back porch of the big house and scurried inside. She sidestepped workers, calling out greetings, and climbed the stairs.

The porch swing beckoned. So what if he'd bought it for her? There was no reason not to enjoy it. Vibrant scarlet, fuchsia, and purple petunias flourished in the boxes Ryler had installed on each side of the railing. Three emerald-winged hummingbirds with splashes of red across their throats flitted about from blossom to blossom. Shell sat and opened the catalog to pick paint colors and decor for each room.

"Hey."

She jumped.

Ryler stood in the doorway of the landing.

"Are you following me?"

"Sort of. I need to ask you something."

"Didn't we already figure out what to do with the flower beds and pick all the fountains?"

"It's not about that."

"If it's not about this place, I don't think we have anything to discuss."

"I have to know." Ryler ran a hand through his hair. "Why did you give him away?"

six

Shell's blood boiled and she jumped up from the swing. "I didn't give him away, and I don't think it's any of your business."

Sucking in a deep breath, Ryler shoved his hands in his pockets. "I need to know and you probably need to talk about it. Would you rather go to your apartment?"

"And have all the workers think. . ." She rolled her eyes. "I wanted Chance—that's my son's name—to have a chance."

"Why couldn't he have a chance with you?"

"His father was Wade Fenwick," she snapped, as if that were a death sentence.

"So?" Ryler shrugged.

"So—" Shell laced the single word with sarcasm. "I didn't want my son raised with the stigma of being the son of the drunk-that-killed-the-preacher's-wife. I was the town slut's daughter, and I'm still trying to live it down."

"I think you're doing a good job."

"You do?" She snorted a derisive laugh. "Two days after we met, I was in your bed." A rare blush warmed her face.

"But you seem different now. You dress different, you look different. More—"

"Respectable."

"That's it." Ryler gently gripped her shoulders. "I don't think anyone thinks of you as the town slut's daughter, and I don't think anyone thought of Wade as the preacher's wife's killer. Grayson officiated his funeral. I think this town, at least that church over there, knows how to forgive and forget."

"Maybe." Her skin tingled at his touch.

Ryler's hands dropped to his sides. "All those weekends I wondered about, when we were together, you were with

91

Chance. I thought you had another man on the side."

"There was never anyone else." *There still isn't.* "My sister managed to rise above our stigma. She and her husband are raising Chance right. In church and in a stable, two-parent family. He's thriving."

"Who are you when you visit?"

"Annie." Her laugh sounded more like a sob. "That's how he pronounces Auntie. I moved to Conway to be close to him and got used to seeing him almost daily. This place, being separated from him, it's killing me."

"What do you say we go to church this week?"

Her gaze met his. "Why?"

"To find out, once and for all, about this Jesus business." He splayed his hands palms up. "Now don't look at me like I've lost my mind. Just think about it. He seems to give people comfort. And it seems you could use some. To be honest, so could I. What do you say?"

Comfort. Could something unseen give her comfort? She'd tried everything else with no results. "I'll think about it."

He gave her shoulder a gentle squeeze and footsteps echoed across the balcony. The door opened and closed.

It took every ounce of willpower she had not to scurry after him.

&

Shell tugged at the dress. Even with the camisole underneath, it wasn't right. Like a second skin and way too short. With a sigh, she wriggled out of it and pulled out her new black dress. People wore black other than to funerals. But her stomach twisted. Wade's coffin, closed with him inside. *Where will you spend eternity?*

With a shiver, she stared at the few dresses she owned. Nothing appropriate. Oh well, she had a good excuse not to go. Except that she'd told Ryler she would.

Shoving hangers aside, she searched for something that wasn't there. A white skirt caught her attention. She must have grabbed one of Savannah's by mistake when she packed.

She pulled it out and held it up. The cottony, gathered

softness would fall mid-calf.

On the hanger next to it, hung an identical skirt in black.

Savannah. Both skirts and a slip had wound up in her suitcase after their discussion of the funeral and how she'd bought a new dress she'd probably never wear again.

Perfect. They were the same size. Shell grabbed the white skirt. Her peach top with a plunging neckline turned respectable with the white camisole underneath. She spun in front of the mirror liking the way the gauzy skirt whirled around her calves.

The doorbell rang. She smoothed her hands over her hair, slipped on high-heel white sandals, and scurried to answer.

"You're going?" Surprise echoed in Ryler's tone.

He looked good in his turquoise polo and black jeans. *Stop looking.*

"I said I would. Just let me grab some jewelry." She hurried to the bedroom. Silver necklace and earrings set off the airy, summery outfit.

Thanks, Savannah. Nice save.

With one more appraisal in the mirror, she hurried back to the living room.

Ryler checked his watch. "We better go, especially if we're walking."

It felt nice being on his arm as they stepped out. The hot sun blazed down on them. Thank goodness her hair was straight. The slight wave she managed to hot roll into it wouldn't last long, but at least it never frizzed.

The charcoal gray Chevy Equinox sat in the drive, next to her car.

"Is that your SUV?"

"Did you think I drove my banged-up work truck all the time?"

"It's all I've ever seen, except for that first day here." She shrugged.

"I always kept the SUV in the garage. I never took you anywhere in it, did I?"

"We usually stayed in." With one thing on their minds.

She cleared her throat. "It's hotter than I realized. Maybe we should have driven. I bet the air-conditioning works great in that nice rig."

"We're almost there now. You look really nice. Like a summer breeze."

"Thanks. My sister loaned me this skirt, but I think I'll keep it." Especially since he liked it.

❧

Ryler tried not to think about how good Shell looked as they stepped inside the church. Maybe he'd take her out for lunch after the service.

He'd never even taken her out to dinner. For three months, she'd spent almost every night with him, but he'd never taken her on a date. No wonder she hadn't loved him. She'd probably felt used. But then she'd used him, too. Could they start over? Could he show her she was more to him than a bed partner?

One excited church member after another greeted them.

With each kind greeting, his insides quaked even more. He wasn't like these people. He might have been if he'd never left home. His parents had been consistent church members. But after they died, he certainly hadn't stayed on the straight and narrow path. He'd never officially been on it.

Finally, the music started and the rush of people headed toward their pews. The harpist trilled her strings. He'd seen the harp during the funeral but assumed it was only for looks. He'd never figured harps existed in a real church. Weren't they just for heaven?

"Ryler, Shell, come sit with us." Sylvie motioned toward Laken, Hayden, Collin, and Brady.

Third pew from the front. Ryler cleared his throat. Shell seemed happy with the offer and took the seat beside Sylvie. He settled on the other side of Shell. If only she knew they were sitting with his family.

He ignored Sylvie and concentrated on Shell. Not hard. Every time one of them moved, her shoulder grazed his.

The worst that could happen, he'd wasted a perfectly

good opportunity to sleep in. But sitting beside Shell might be worth it. Her maddening perfume, sparkling eyes, and curtain of blond hair filled his thoughts.

As a congregational hymn began, Shell grabbed a book out of the rack in front of them and sang along. Her soft soprano melted him further. *Amazing Grace.*

A rush of memories crashed around him—sitting between his parents, singing hymns, the sermons, Sunday school class. His dad explaining salvation to him. Feeling loved. By his parents and by Someone bigger. He'd been on the verge of giving in to that love when they'd told him the truth. But then he'd turned his back. And after they died, he'd turned his back on God, too.

When the second verse began, Shell turned the page, then with a frown, flipped back to the original.

Pointing to the next verse below the first, he showed her the right place. She started singing again.

The song ended and Pastor Grayson stepped to the pulpit and opened his Bible. "Turn with me to John 10:10."

Pages flipped and rustled as Ryler's heart raced.

" 'The thief cometh not, but for to steal, and to kill, and to destroy: I am come that they might have life, and that they might have it more abundantly.' "

The pastor said a prayer and then continued. "I don't know why bad things happen in this world. I don't know why kids are neglected, abused, abandoned, or orphaned. I don't know why families have a falling-out and never see one another again. I don't know why some folks live to a ripe old age and some folks get cut short."

Ryler swallowed.

"I don't know why tragedies and disasters happen. I don't have the answers. But what I do know is that no matter what happens in this world, God can get you through it. I'm living proof. Four years ago, I was at my lowest."

The message sank into Ryler's soul. Everyone had problems, traumas, and issues. Shell, the pastor, Collin. Even his parents had struggled with three miscarriages. While he and Shell dwelled on pain and the past, Grayson and Collin had moved forward. They didn't dwell on the bad stuff. His parents hadn't either.

"My first wife died with me sitting right beside her." Pastor Sterling paced behind the pulpit. "Helpless. I was eaten up with grief, but I had a son to raise. God gave me the strength and, when I was ready, He brought Adrea into my life. What a blessing she's been to Dayne and me. And now we have a new little girl to cherish.

"A few weeks ago, I preached the funeral for the man who accidentally killed Sara. Four years ago, I'd have never dreamed I'd have the strength to do such a thing."

The people in this church gave their pain to God, like Ryler's parents had. He'd had eighteen awesome years, then turned bitter and blamed God. He could have had a lifetime of woe. And he still had a whole other set of parents he could get to know. If he could only muster the courage to tell them who he was. Maybe Sylvie had changed. Maybe Martin could get help.

"If you have loved ones who've passed away and they were Christians, you can see them again. Accept Jesus. His truth will set you free." Pastor Grayson finished his altar plea.

Ryler could barely stay seated until the music began. He rose to step around Shell, but she made the first move. He followed her.

At the altar they both knelt. Soon Pastor Grayson joined Shell, while Mark knelt with Ryler.

"Do you want to accept Jesus, Ryler?"

"Yes." Ryler's voice quivered as joy swooshed through him. "And I understand salvation. My parents were Christians."

"All right, then. Just stay until you're finished. I won't bother you." Mark stepped away.

"Dear God, I'm sorry for breaking my parents' hearts. I'm sorry for turning my back on You, and ignoring You. Forgive me for the mess I've made of my life. Help me to turn it around, to rely on You for strength and to live the way my parents would have wanted me to. Mold me into a new creature. Be with Shell and me, Lord. If we're right together, give me strength to treat her like a lady and honor her.

"Help me find the grace You've shown me in dealing with my biological parents, Lord. Help me to honor them. Most of all, thank You for dying on the cross for me. Thank You for saving my soul." He stood and wiped the tears from his face.

Sylvie and Laken knelt at the altar also, along with Collin and Hayden. Tears streamed down the women's faces. Praying to find Him? Praying for their father? Probably a bit of both.

Shell was already standing in their row again, singing along with the hymn "Have Thine Own Way, Lord." Her eyes glistened and a tremulous smile lifted the corners of her lips. As a few others lingered at the altar, she held the hymnal so he could see. Her other hand rested on the pew in front of her. Thankful they'd made such a monumental decision together, he covered her hand with his.

❧

The last of the church members wished them well and left. Still in the sanctuary, Shell turned to Ryler. "I can't believe I did that. I didn't even want to go to church today."

"But aren't you glad you did?"

She nodded. "I had no idea what to do or say. Grayson had to explain everything and he even said the prayer for me. I just repeated it in my head and at the moment, I don't understand anything. My brain is spinning." The man who was hurt most by her and Wade's antics had led her to Christ. Her vision blurred.

"You don't have to understand, as long as you accept His grace. You'll understand more as you keep attending church and read your Bible."

"You seem to know all about it."

"Not all about it, but my parents were Christians. I was in church until I was eighteen."

"I only went to church maybe six months out of my whole life and it seems like a lifetime ago."

"Just stick around and you'll catch on." Ryler linked his fingers with hers. "You got any of those leftover sandwiches Grace sent over yesterday?"

"Two or three. I tried to get you to take them."

"Let's go on a picnic."

Pastor Grayson and Adrea stood inside the lobby door as the last of the congregation trickled outside.

"I'd be glad to answer any questions anytime." Adrea hugged her.

She seemed so sincere. How could someone forgive so completely?

"At this point, I don't even know what to ask."

"Just know I'm willing to talk."

"We'll set up a meeting soon and talk about baptism, too." Grayson shook their hands. "We're really glad y'all came this morning, and please come back."

They strolled out the door and across the street, with her hand tucked in his elbow.

"I'll run home and change. I thought we'd have a picnic at the park. Do you want to meet me there or at my place?"

"I don't know where your place is." She leaned against his side as her heel wobbled on the gravel drive.

"I'm on Highway 5, number 124."

Shell shivered. Across from Wade's old house.

"Are you cold?" Ryler frowned. "It's got to be at least ninety degrees."

"I'm fine. I'll meet you at the park." She never wanted to see Wade's house ever again. Not even from across the street.

"All right. See you there and don't forget the sandwiches. I'll bring snacks and drinks."

❧

Birds chirped and sang as Ryler spread a fuzzy taupe blanket on the wildflower carpet of purple, yellow, and white. His muscled arms rippled with each movement.

Find something else to look at. Shell turned away from him.

A few families dotted the park, but they'd chosen a secluded corner behind a large sycamore tree.

She emptied the sacks they'd brought. "This would be the perfect picnic if we had one of those wicker picnic baskets like you see in the movies."

"The food's just as good from a brown paper sack." He handed her a bottled sweet tea. "This morning can change our lives. It's like a do-over. Our pasts are forgiven. We get a new chance to live differently."

"A fresh start."

A couple rounded the walking path, hand in hand.

"Can I ask you something?"

"I won't promise to answer."

"Fair enough. Why did you break things off when I asked you to move in with me?"

Shell swallowed hard. *Because I was falling for you, so I thought I'd leave before you got the chance to leave me.* "I wasn't looking for. . ."

"Mr. Forever. Just Mr. Right Now. Same here, only Ms. of course. But it didn't work out that way for me. I didn't mean to fall for you, but I did and this job brought you back into my life." He took her hands in his. "My feelings haven't lessened, Shell. And I don't want you to walk away again."

Why hadn't he told her that then? Could she trust him with forever? Her mouth went dry.

"You don't have to say anything." He drew her into his arms. "I haven't been with anyone since you."

Me neither.

His kiss was soft and tender, as if he treasured her. Not about sex. Dizzy, she leaned against him for support. Despite the gentle, undemanding caress of his lips, fire swept through her veins as it always had when she was in his arms.

With a groan, he pulled away enough to gaze into her eyes. "I want to do things right."

"Right?"

"We can't have sex."

"Huh?"

"We're Christians now. God created sex for marriage only. I want to live right. The way my parents raised me to live."

He grabbed his Bible. Sitting cross-legged, Ryler kicked off his shoes. His knee-length shorts revealed muscled calves.

Concentrate on the Bible.

He flipped through the pages. "Here it is. First Corinthians 6:18–20."

Shell sat next to him, head huddled close to his and read along with him.

" 'Flee fornication. Every sin that a man doeth is without the body; but he that committeth fornication sinneth against his own body. What? know ye not that your body is the temple of the Holy Ghost which is in you, which ye have of God, and ye are not your own?' "

The text blurred as hot tears filled her eyes. "How do you know where to find stuff?"

"My youth pastor drilled this into our brains. And before I moved from Little Rock, I visited with my aunt. Our visit got me thinking about where I came from. Since then, I've been reading the Bible."

"Go on, read more."

" 'For ye are bought with a price: therefore glorify God in your body, and in your spirit, which are God's.' What it's saying is that every sin is outside the body, except for premarital sex, which is a sin against our own bodies. When we became Christians, the Holy Spirit entered into us."

She cringed at the places her body had been. "So, everything we do with our bodies, we're taking Jesus with us."

"And we were bought by the blood He shed on the cross for our sins, so whatever we do, we should glorify Him. Sort of like making Him proud or doing things that lets other people see His love inside us."

"I don't think I've ever done anything that would make Him proud." Shell shook her head.

"But we've got a clean slate." He squeezed her hand. "Today, we start over."

"Thanks for showing me. I'm glad you know all this stuff." She drew away from him a bit. If she could get far enough away, maybe she could resist him. *Yeah, right.*

"I was on the verge of accepting Jesus as my Savior before I left home."

"Why didn't you? It seems like you'd have needed Him more than ever after your parents' deaths. You were all alone."

"You're right, but instead, I turned my back on God. For a long time, I refused to care about anyone. Until you."

She wanted to tell him she felt the same way, but would he stick around? No other man in her life ever had.

"I want us to be honest with each other. Starting with the reason I left home." He took a deep breath. "My parents told me I was adopted."

Shell gasped. "After eighteen years, I bet that was quite a bomb."

"I wish they'd just told me from the beginning."

She leaned her forehead against his shoulder. Offer comfort without seducing him. "Maybe they wanted you to feel you truly belonged with them."

"Whatever their reasons, I shouldn't have left."

"Do you know where your biological parents are?"

His jaw tensed.

"You should try to find them. You've got a whole other family out there somewhere. You don't have to be alone."

He stiffened and pulled away from her. "Just replace the parents who died with another set? Like buying a new car."

"That's not what I meant."

"Good." The word came through clenched teeth. "Because my parents could never be replaced." Ryler stood.

She jumped to her feet. "I just meant—you might even have siblings."

"Riley and Loretta Grant are my parents. I don't need another set because I had perfection." He ran a hand through his hair and stalked toward his SUV. "But I didn't realize it until it was too late."

"Ryler, wait."

He didn't even turn around.

Shoulders slumped, she sank back to the blanket.

No, he wouldn't stick around. He was like all the rest. One wrong word, one wrong gesture, one wrong question, and they bolted. Like a racehorse, but in the wrong direction. Away from her.

❧

The porch swing stopped. Shell pushed off with one foot to set it swaying again. Paint fumes burned her nasal passages, even out here. The nonexistent breeze of early June didn't help matters. With all the doors and windows open, surely the smell wouldn't last long.

The reds, golds, and sage tones she'd chosen gave each room a romantic, soft feel with their billowy curtains and sleek antique furnishings. The rest of the furniture would arrive next week, with the bedspreads to follow. Then the final touches of mirrors, paintings, and wall hangings. It was all coming together quite nicely.

Except for the constant distraction named Ryler. A week had passed since their argument and they'd barely spoken two words to each other since.

"Hey, Shell."

How did he always do that? Call her name, just when she was thinking about him.

She stood and stepped over to the railing.

Covered in dirt, he looked better than any clean man had a right to, despite the frown marring his forehead.

"What?"

"My helper won't be here today, and I can't find anyone to replace him."

She closed her eyes. So close to completion. So close to going home to Chance. So close to leaving Ryler behind.

"I've already set the date for the grand opening." Even though Darrell conveniently hadn't found a manager yet. She threw her hands up. "I've called Grace about the food and ordered the flowers from Adrea. This place has to be finished, including that monstrosity of a waterfall. If I have to do it myself, it will be done on time."

His frown grew more intense. "Glad you feel that way. You better go put on some clothes you don't mind ruining."

"Huh?" Her mouth moved, but nothing else came out. She propped her hands on her hips. "I didn't really mean—" She sighed. But if it would get this job finished. . . "I'll be right there."

She hurried down the stairs and out the back door to her apartment. Something she didn't mind ruining. . . She pulled her most faded jeans from the hamper. Yesterday, she'd accidentally leaned her hip into a freshly painted wall. They'd do.

The oversized T-shirt she slept in, with an old iron-on mostly peeled off, and grass-stained tennis shoes completed the lovely outfit. She pulled her hair into a high ponytail.

Ryler's mouth flattened into a thin line when he saw her. "You look like a teenager with your hair like that. Very fitting."

Whatever. "What do you need me to do?"

"If you'll dig the holes, I'll wrestle the rocks in." He handed her a trowel, careful not to touch her.

"Okay, how deep?"

"Not very. See this rock?" He flipped over a flat boulder, half the size of him, with ease.

"It's thicker on one end." He strode past her. "It's going right here. I need this area dug out, so it's level. You might break a nail."

She rolled her eyes and jabbed the trowel in the ground inches from his foot. "I'll live."

"If you stab my foot, I won't be able to finish the job on time."

And she'd have to put up with him longer.

Tension roiled in the humid air as Ryler left her to digging and started on the other side. As far as he could get, away from her.

&

The stiff cleaning brush Shell usually used on the bathtub would surely scrub the hide from her fingers. She added more soap. Still a line of embedded soil remained under the few nails she had left.

Pounding at the door made her jump.

Drying her hands, she hurried to peer through the peephole.

Ryler.

"Shell, can I come in? I've been thinking about what you said last week. About contacting my parents."

She jerked the door open. "And?"

Clean and shaven, he'd changed into fresh jeans and a hunter green T-shirt that strained over his shoulder muscles.

"I'm sorry I stormed off like that." He paced her small living room. "You were only trying to help."

"It doesn't matter."

"Yes, it does." He strode over to her. "I still want that future with you. Just know it will include my temper."

Gently, he gripped her shoulders. "Can we talk?"

Her breath stalled. "I'm not sure. Lately, every time I talk, you bite my head off."

"I'm sorry." He hung his head. "Being adopted—it's a sore subject with me. It reminds me of how badly I hurt my parents when I left, and now I feel guilty even thinking about contacting my biological parents."

All her anger evaporated. "Like you're replacing them, you said. How did the Grants feel about your biological parents? Do you know?"

"My aunt gave me a letter they wrote in case anything ever happened to them. They wanted me to find my family, so I wouldn't be alone."

She cupped his cheek in her hand. "So what do you have to feel guilty about?"

"My biological family lives in this area. That's why I came to Searcy and that's why I moved to Romance."

Her eyes widened. "Here? Do you know who they are?"

The muscles in his throat flexed. "The Krofts."

She gasped and her jaw dropped. "Oh, Ryler. They don't know who you are."

"I moved to Searcy to decide whether to reveal my identity.

Or not." He ran his hand through his hair. "And to tell you the truth, when I first met Sylvie, I decided not. But then I learned I had siblings."

Her gaze dropped to his massive chest. "So you moved to Romance."

"To watch them from afar."

"That's why you invited me to Laken's dinner party." Her eyes met his. "It wasn't about me."

"If it wasn't about you"—he grinned—"I'd have gone alone. But I wanted to make sure you didn't get a date with anyone else. Who knew you had a past with my brother?"

She rolled her eyes. "Nothing happened."

"Yeah, but he wanted it to."

"Not anymore." She traced his jaw with her thumb, his nearness working on her pulse. "Ryler, you have to tell them. Have you decided?"

"I have. I think you're right. Sylvie has changed." He captured her hand and pressed his lips to her fingertips then leaned his forehead against hers. "Will you come with me to tell them?"

She shivered and all resistance she possessed dissolved. "Only if you'll kiss me again. It might help me decide."

He backed up. One brow lifted. "Decide what?"

"Whether we might have a future? Or not?"

His lips sought hers. Again, soft, sweet, and gentle. Like no kiss she'd ever known.

A kiss to savor and remember. Because she'd already decided.

Even as his kiss melted her into a puddle at his feet, she knew.

He was a Kroft and Shell Evans didn't run in the same circles as the Krofts. She'd go with him to tell his family—offer him strength, but there could be no future for them. From her disreputable beginnings and sordid past, she couldn't span the gulf between them. Ryler Grant's past was a bit sordid, too, but his blood ran in the right circles. Even though his mother had befriended her, they weren't of the same class. And they never would be.

❧

Ryler looked toward the porch ceiling and rolled his neck from side to side, grinding tendons against tensed muscle.

"It'll be fine." Shell squeezed his hand. "You're doing the right thing."

"I'm glad you came with me." Beside him, at the most important crossroad in his life. *Lord, give me strength.*

"Me, too. I can't wait to see Sylvie's face. She'll be so happy."

"You don't think she'll be disappointed? I mean—I'm not polished and savvy like Collin." He raised his arms. "Even in this ridiculous sports coat. I should have worn my jeans, like I usually do."

"You look better than Collin could ever hope to look." She straightened his collar. "You're real and you're her son. That's all she'll care about. Want me to ring the bell?"

"Could you?"

She jabbed the button. "But I won't tell them. You have to do that yourself."

Wanting to bolt, Ryler closed his eyes. Run. Squeal tires out of here and never come back.

The door opened and Hayden frowned. "Ryler, is everything all right?"

"Fine. Is everyone here?"

Shell squeezed his hand again.

"Yes. And very curious." Hayden stepped aside so they could enter. "But I'm afraid Mr. Kroft won't be coming down. He isn't feeling well."

Drunk. Ryler's gut twisted and he tried to concentrate on the decor. Classy and expensive, but not over the top. It still didn't make sense. If he had a trust fund, then Collin and Laken likely did, too, yet Martin and Sylvie's home wasn't overly grand or ostentatious. Had Martin drank away the fortune? And where had the money come from to begin with?

"They're waiting in the drawing—I mean the den. Right through here." Hayden tapped on the door, then swung it open. "Your guest has arrived—with a guest."

Sylvie sat on a throne-like white chair. Hayden claimed a seat beside Laken on the matching couch, and Collin sat in the twin chair.

"Why, Shell, what a pleasant surprise." Sylvie's brows drew together. "Ryler, it's always nice to see you, but I must admit, I'm confused as to what this meeting could possibly be about."

Sucking in a deep breath, Ryler paused. Where to start? He fished in the inside pocket of his sports coat. "It's about"—pulling out her letter and the pearls, he held them up dangling from his trembling fingers—"these."

seven

With a gasp, Sylvie jumped up. "Where did you get those?"

Ryler swallowed the taste of bile rising in his throat. "Out of my safe deposit box."

"You're"—Sylvie's chin quivered—"our son?"

Laken clasped a hand over her mouth.

Closing his eyes, Collin grinned, as if to say, *Why didn't I figure it out sooner?*

"Hayden, Collin, go get Martin." Sylvie tried to blink away tears. "Bring him down even if you have to carry him."

"Now, wait a minute." Hayden put a protective arm around Laken's waist. "I don't mean to seem ugly, but how do we know if Ryler is the real deal? For all we know, he could have stolen the key or found it in the trash."

"I know." A sob escaped Sylvie and she pressed her knuckles against her trembling lips. "I should have known the moment I saw him. Maybe a part of me did. He's Martin made over, as a young man. Except for the facial structure and the eyes, which I see every day in my mirror."

Ryler felt like a child as they talked around him. *I'm right here in the room.*

"I'm sorry." Hayden shook his head. "I certainly don't mean to steal the potential joy out of the situation, but I think we need proof before we tell Martin. If this is a mistake, it might kill him."

"It's no hoax." Ryler's jaw clenched. "I have a letter from my birth parents telling me who my biological parents are. I have twenty thousand dollars, which I haven't spent a penny of, that I found in my safe deposit box with Sylvie's letter and the pearls. I'd be happy to take a blood test."

"That's not necessary." Collin shook his head. "Mother's right. Look at him."

"You've been in town for months." Hayden rubbed his stubbled jaw. "Why are you just now telling us who you are?"

Ryler's Adam's apple worked. "I wasn't sure I wanted to be a part of this family. Parents who gave me away. Siblings who possibly didn't know I existed."

"We didn't give you up by choice." Sylvie's voice shook.

"I'm sorry, Sylvie, I'm only trying to protect this family."

"Protect this family or your share of the inheritance?" Ryler's tone had a steely edge to it.

"I'll never touch Laken's money," Hayden growled.

"Stop it." Laken's voice cracked. "This isn't getting us anywhere."

Sylvie patted Hayden's arm. "I know you're worried, but I'm convinced. Ryler has Martin's hair, my features, and my grandmother's pearls. We'll have a paternity test before we tell Martin, but it's a technicality. Now, please leave us. I'd like to speak with my son. Alone."

"You okay?" Shell whispered.

He closed his eyes and squeezed her hand. "I need to speak with Shell. I'll be back."

His wobbly legs worked well enough to get him outside. "I'm fine. Thanks for being here, but I guess I'll do this part on my own."

"I'll wait here."

"It's hot and this could take awhile. Go on home." He handed Shell the keys to his SUV and kissed her temple. "If it goes long, go home. I'm sure Collin would take me by your place to pick up my rig."

The door opened and Collin came out, followed by Hayden and Laken.

Collin punched his shoulder. "I should have known. Welcome to the clan, bro."

The brothers bumped fists.

With a sniffle, Laken flew into his arms. "I'm glad you're here. Don't mind Hayden, he's just concerned."

"Someone has to keep on top of the emotion." Hayden offered his hand. "But for the record, I believe you."

"No hard feelings." Ryler shook hands with his brother-in-law. "We'll do the blood test and put everyone's minds at ease. And for the record, I'm not here for the money. I'd just like to know my family."

Laken pulled away and gave his shoulder a squeeze. "I'm so thankful you're home."

"Me, too. I think."

"We're going to hang out in the family room if you'd like to join us, Shell." Collin opened the door.

"Thanks, but I'm fine here."

"Please. . ." Laken hesitated at the door. "Join us, Shell."

"I need some fresh air."

They went back inside, leaving only Shell still there for support.

"You should wait inside with them. They don't bite."

"Collin might. Go." She sat in a chair at the table on the porch. "I'll be right here."

He blew her a kiss and stepped back inside.

Sylvie met him in the entryway. "I was so afraid you wouldn't come back." She lunged into him with a hug.

His arms remained at his sides as a flurry of emotions warred within him.

"I'm sorry." A woman's confused voice came from his left.

Sylvie jerked away.

The maid stood in the dining area. "Excuse me, ma'am. Will you and your guest need anything?"

"Yes. I'd like a lovely glass of sweet tea. What about you, Ryler?"

"That sounds great." Maybe it would dislodge his tongue.

"We'll be in the den. And please tell Martin I still have guests." She tucked her hand in his elbow, as if they were old friends. They retraced their steps.

After shutting the double doors behind them, she sat on the couch. "Ryler, I want you to know we didn't throw you away. And Martin and I have never made any arrangements for what would happen if you didn't claim your inheritance." She patted the seat beside her. "Hayden loves this family and he's only watching out for us. Please don't hold it against him."

"He's protective of his family. I can respect that." He took a seat at the other end of the couch, clasping his hands in front of him. "Why did you give me away?"

"I was sixteen when I met Martin." A heavy sigh came from deep within her. "My family didn't like him because he came from the wrong side of the tracks, so to speak. You see, I come from a very well-to-do family. The kind of people who have mansions and hordes of servants. The kind of people who look down on the ordinary working class."

"They didn't want you involved with someone beneath you." Ryler frowned.

"They wouldn't even let me see him." Sylvie dabbed her eyes with a tissue, her bracelets jingling with each movement. "My parents threatened to cut me out of the family fortune if I didn't stop seeing him."

"But you didn't stop."

"No. Money had nothing to do with how Martin and I felt about each other. For the first time in my life, money didn't matter. We snuck around, stealing time together whenever we could. Many nights, I snuck out of my bedroom."

"And you got pregnant."

Sylvie's eyes closed. "Martin begged my parents to let him marry me. You can imagine how horrified they were. Not only had I been sneaking around behind their backs, but I was pregnant by a commoner. They whisked me off to Little Rock before anyone found out, hoping to save the family name. And they gave me two choices." Her voice broke. "Abortion or adoption."

A hard swallow couldn't dislodge the boulder in his throat.

A knock sounded at the door. "Your tea is ready, ma'am."

"Come in, Sharlene. Just leave the pitcher here and please see that we're not interrupted, except when the nurse arrives."

His father required a nurse?

"Yes, ma'am."

"Thank you, dear." Sylvie took a sip of her tea.

Ryler drained his glass and set it back on the coffee table.

"My, you were parched." She poured him another glass.

"I guess I should thank you for letting me live."

More tears filled her eyes. "I never considered anything else. I begged and pleaded, but my parents wouldn't budge. I chose life for you."

But without her and Martin in it.

"As soon as I turned eighteen, I came back to Searcy and married Martin. We wanted to find you, but my parents cut me off and we didn't have the money to hire a lawyer. We tried to get on with our lives, to move forward. We had Collin and then Laken, but there was always a Martin Jr.-sized hole in our family and in our hearts. But you know most of this from my letter."

Pressure built up in his chest, as if he might explode. "I never read the bulk of it. Just the beginning and your names."

"Why?" A frown creased her forehead.

"No offense, but I already had parents."

Her hand shook as she sipped her tea. "Finally, when you were six, my grandmother gave me my trust fund. We hired a lawyer, which led us to the children's home in Little Rock. But by then, you'd been adopted. The director assured us that you were in a good, stable Christian home."

Ryler swallowed.

"Martin and I cried and prayed over the decision and came to the conclusion that we couldn't rip you away from everything you'd ever known. Were you happy with your adoptive family?"

"My parents were awesome." Weird discussing his parents with his mother.

Her mouth twitched.

"Sorry. It must be odd for you to hear."

"No, I so hoped you were happy and loved. I'm glad you were. Do they know you found me?"

"They died shortly after I turned eighteen."

"Oh my." Sylvie clasped a hand over her mouth. "I'm so sorry. Did you know you were adopted?"

He nodded. Why go into the rest of it? "My aunt gave me the key after their funeral, but I wasn't emotionally ready to deal with any of it. She insisted I had to open the box by my thirtieth birthday."

Her chin quivered. "Since my parents set up trust funds for Laken and Collin, Martin and I used most of my inheritance to set up your trust. We put the pearls and the money in the safe deposit box and lived on my shares Grandmother left me in the family company. The director of the children's home promised to give the key to your"—Sylvie swallowed hard—"parents.

"Over the years, we longed for you. Sometimes my arms literally ached, I wanted to hold you so badly. I so wish we could have raised you. Everything would have been so different."

But he'd had a blessed childhood and didn't regret a moment of his time with the Grants. Meeting his biological mother still felt like a betrayal to them, yet it was what they wanted. Tangled emotions bubbled inside him.

"Instead, I coped by becoming a snooty busybody, while Martin started drinking and it steadily got worse and worse. He's better. As your thirtieth birthday approached, we hoped your adoptive parents would give you the trust fund papers. It gave us hope."

A loud gong. Ryler jumped as the grandfather clock gonged five more times. They'd been at this an hour. No wonder he was exhausted.

He gulped another swig of tea. "What do you mean, he's better? Is he getting treatment?"

"No, but for the first time ever, he's thinking about it." Sylvie pinched the pleat of her slacks between her thumb and forefinger. "But I think the possibility that you might come home made him realize he has a problem. He doesn't want you to see what losing you did to him. We've all been going through the motions of life, waiting for you."

Hearing her side of the story seemed so surreal. For twelve years, he'd hated the mother he thought had abandoned him.

Only to learn she was forced into it. "You wanted me?"

"More than anything. From the moment I realized you were there." She pressed a hand to her stomach.

Ryler moved over beside her and hugged her. "You're not angry that I didn't tell you who I was sooner?"

"I'm just glad you're here. Welcome home, son." She trembled, sobbing into his shoulder.

A knock sounded. "Ma'am, the nurse is here."

"Give us a moment, then send her in." Sylvie reluctantly pulled away from him, dabbing at her eyes with a tissue.

"Are you ill?"

"I took the liberty of calling for a paternity test. Don't worry. It doesn't even require blood anymore. They stick some sort of swab in your mouth. And the results will be back in three days."

"Sounds painless enough."

She cupped his cheek in her hand. "For the record, I know exactly who you are, but this will ease everyone's concerns and it wouldn't hurt to have proof in hand in order to get your adoption records open so that you can claim the trust fund."

"But I don't want the money."

"Well, it really doesn't matter. It's your money. Now don't look a gift horse in the mouth, and prepare to be swabbed." She patted his cheek. "So handsome. Just like your father."

A tap sounded on the door.

"Come in."

The double doors opened and a nurse dressed in a scrub uniform entered.

≈

Why had a nurse been summoned? Unease grew in the pit of Shell's stomach until she was as jittery as the sycamore leaves dropping from early June's heat-scorched trees. The rapidly darkening sky cooled the evening air only slightly.

The door opened and she jumped up.

Ryler looked as if the faint breeze could knock him over, but the hurt in his eyes had eased a bit.

"You okay?"

"I can't believe you're still here."

"I told you I'd stay."

He checked his watch. "But that was over an hour ago."

"Why did the nurse come?"

"Paternity test."

"Sylvie doesn't believe you."

"No, she believes me, but she wants to make sure everyone else does."

"So, you didn't see your father?"

"No. She's with him now, making up some excuse about strep throat so the nurse can get his DNA." He took her elbow and steered her down the steps. "Let's go."

"You're ready?"

"Sylvie wanted me to stay, but I need to process everything I learned." He ran a shaky hand through his hair. "I can't absorb anything else today."

"If you don't mind me driving your SUV, you can relax on the ride home."

"Just what the doctor ordered. I never knew life could be so exhausting."

"Are you and Sylvie okay?"

"We're good and the test will come back in three days. We're not telling anyone who I am until then." He entwined his fingers with hers.

"I've been wondering, will you go by Martin Jr. or Ryler?"

"Definitely Ryler."

"Good. You don't seem like Junior and Ryler is a really cool name."

As they climbed into his steamy vehicle, he punched the air-conditioning to blast off, and leaned his head back against the rest. "Thanks. I was named after my dad—the other one."

Shell concentrated on the traffic until they were out of the city limits, then stole a glance at him. Fast asleep.

❧

Despite the previous evening's turmoil, Ryler had slept hard, and three cups of coffee later, he was still bleary-eyed.

Why, Lord? He gripped the steering wheel harder, navigating the hills between Romance and Rose Bud without even thinking. Why did he feel so guilty? Torn between two families?

The past didn't matter now. It couldn't be changed. He'd lean on God to see him through. And Shell.

She cared about him. For whatever reason, she couldn't bring herself to admit it, but he was almost certain she loved him.

Flipping his blinker on, he waited for the oncoming vehicles to pass, then turned into the bed-and-breakfast. It was beginning to look like one, with sparkling glass in every window, fresh balcony railing, and newly painted pristine siding. With the exterior complete, a few finishing touches inside remained.

The grounds were taking shape. Flowers and rosebushes flourished now, with only the front fountain and a few walkways left to finish.

His gaze rose to the balcony.

At the railing, Shell's eyes riveted on him.

A smile reached his soul. He waved, jumped out of the truck, and jogged to the big house.

Up the main staircase, he took two steps at a time.

At the landing on the second floor, she waited. "You okay?"

"I am. Sorry I conked out on you during the drive home last night." He cleared his throat and glanced at the workers nearby. The steady hum of power tools with hisses, ticks, and booms covered their conversation. But just in case, he steered her toward the swing.

She settled on the left. "You were emotionally exhausted. With good reason. I was worried you'd fall asleep driving to your place."

Claiming the other end of the swing, he kept his distance. Nothing to stir gossip among the carpenters. He'd once worsened her reputation, but from now on, he'd honor Shell, not sully her.

"I've never felt so torn in my life." Leaning forward, he cradled his head in his hands. "In a way, I wish I could have been raised by Martin and Sylvie, with my brother and sister. Sylvie would have been a better person and spared countless lives from gossip. And Martin might never have become an alcoholic."

"It's normal to feel that way."

"But it's a betrayal to my parents."

"It's not, Ryler." She rubbed his back in soothing circles. "It's a difficult situation. If Sylvie had given you up because she didn't want you, it would be different. But this way, you wouldn't be human if you didn't wonder 'what if?'"

He straightened up. "You're right. And I am oh, so human." Human enough that her touch electrified him. He leaned back, forcing her to move her hand and stop the havoc her comfort wreaked.

"Have you heard from any of your new family?"

"I'm having supper with Sylvie tonight at Colton's over in Searcy. Hayden called and apologized again for being suspicious of me."

"Your willingness to take the paternity test must have convinced him."

"Tomorrow night, I'm having dinner at Laken and Hayden's with Collin and Sylvie. I was hoping you'd join me."

"Absolutely not."

He frowned. "Why?"

"You need time with your family—alone. Especially with your mother."

"My mother." He ran his fingers through his hair. "It's weird. My mom died twelve years ago." And now, he had a new one.

"She won't try to replace your mother."

"I know, it's just weird. And even though I know who I am, Hayden said something that bothered me."

"What?"

"What if my papers got mixed up at the children's home? What if I'm not Martin Rothwell Kroft?"

Shell's eyebrow lifted. "Rothwell? Oh, I think you definitely look like a Rothwell. I think I'll call you that from now on."

He grinned. "Try it and I won't answer. It was Sylvie's maiden name. Seriously, what if?"

"You've got her eyes. The very thing that first attracted me to you. I mean—well, you knew I was attracted to you. Obviously."

Ryler captured her hand. "Come with me to dinner at Laken's tomorrow night."

"You're a big boy. You can handle it. Alone. And besides, we're having dinner with Grayson and Adrea the next night, so I'll see you then. When do you get the test results?"

"Friday afternoon." He'd need a distraction. "Let's take half the day off and run away. Do something distracting."

"Such as?" She scooted closer to him and laid her head against his shoulder.

He laughed. "Nothing sinful."

≈

Grayson and Adrea's large home reminded Shell of the B & B, but it wasn't as old. Large rooms and high ceilings gave it a spacious feel, yet Adrea had kept it cozy with warm furnishings and family pictures. After supper, Grayson, Dayne, and Ryler cleaned the kitchen, while Shell followed her unlikely hostess to the living room for coffee.

Adrea settled on the couch, cradling a cooing Ashley on one shoulder.

Might as well get it over with. Shell chose a chair across from Adrea and cleared her throat. "I've meant to tell you something. I'm sorry for hurting you." That sounded weak. *More like, I did my level best to destroy your life.*

Adrea closed her eyes for a moment. "It's all in the past."

"Yes, but I am sorry. I wasn't for a long time. In fact, I gloated about it." Wade had been a game to her. "I'd seen you with Wade around Searcy and you were the kind of woman I'd always wanted to be. Upstanding, moral, classy. . . I couldn't be, so I thought it was fun to steal your fiancé. I don't know how you can ever forgive me."

Adrea patted Ashley's back in a steady rhythm. "I was hurt by what happened and for a time, I was very bitter. But I turned it over to God. Once I did that, I got past the bitterness and got on with my life. Then, I could see your pain."

Shell shook her head. "Poor Wade got caught in the middle and I led him to his doom."

"Wade made his own decisions and you couldn't make him do anything he wasn't willing to do. I just wish he hadn't hurt himself or anyone else." Adrea stared off into space for a moment then readjusted Ashley on her other shoulder.

Oh, to hold Chance whenever she wanted. On a daily basis, part of her life. She hugged herself.

"So did Grayson answer all your questions about baptism?"

"Yes. I can't believe how my life is turning around."

Adrea smiled. "You have a new chance to be upstanding, moral, and classy. I never thought of myself as classy, but thanks for the compliment."

"Maybe the moral part, but I don't feel upstanding or classy."

"We need to work on your self-image." Adrea stood, grabbed her hand, and dragged her to a large gilded mirror. "Look at yourself. What do you see?"

Shell stared into her own blue eyes, at the natural-looking blond hair, the modest clothing. "I see a bimbo trying to pretend she's someone else."

"Oh, Shell. You're beautiful. Inside and out. Look at yourself the way God sees you. You're innocent and precious in His sight. Made in His image, a daughter of God, and co-heir of Christ."

"I don't feel worthy."

"He sees you as worthy. When you humbled yourself to accept Jesus as your Savior, you became worthy. You have to let go of the past, Shell. He has."

Shell took a deep breath and closed her eyes. Let go of the past. If only she could.

❧

Cleaning the kitchen reminded Ryler of helping his mother.

With a final swipe across the countertop, Grayson dumped the dishcloth into the sink and sat at the table. "Dayne, you may go play with Cocoa now."

"Thanks, Dad. See you later, Mr. Ryler." The boy launched out the back door and excited barks greeted him.

Ryler claimed the chair across from Grayson. "I'm having a problem, Preacher."

"What's that?"

"Well, you see, Shell and I, we knew each other before. And now things are different and. . ."

"Whatever you tell me goes no further, but"—Grayson grinned—"I'm no good at fill-in-the-blank."

Ryler sucked in a deep breath. "We had a relationship for about three months and we were. . .intimate. On more than one occasion. My fault completely." Not completely, but he'd gladly save what he could of Shell's rep by taking the blame. "We haven't"—he cleared his throat—"done anything since we ended up working together here, but we've had a couple of close calls."

"And now you're both saved, but you still want to be intimate."

"Well no, I mean not really. We know it's wrong. We don't want to."

"But your flesh does." Grayson cupped his chin in one hand, leaning an elbow on the table.

"Definitely. We've read verses together. Shell—she hasn't had much church, so I showed her some verses on fornication. She didn't even know what it meant."

"It's good that you're reading the Bible together." Grayson nodded. "A very good start. And it's awesome that you want to live differently now. It never ceases to amaze me how unmarried people who get saved in the morning can go to bed with their significant other that night, just like they did the night before."

"But the Bible says it's wrong."

"You're right. I don't know if they don't realize that, they don't care, or they don't think it applies to them because they've already been intimate. Anyway, I'm impressed with both of you."

Ryler ran his hand through his hair. "Every time she's near, I want to throw her over my shoulder like some Neanderthal, haul her up the stairs of the B & B, and love her for the rest of my days." Ryler winced. "I mean emotionally."

"Of course." Grayson laughed. "And physically."

"Sorry, that was probably too much information."

"It's okay. I'm human, too."

"But what do I do about it?"

"You keep coming to church, keep reading the Bible together, and pray about it." Grayson sipped his coffee. "Don't have dinner at her place or yours. Take her out in public. Don't stop somewhere secluded to sit in the car and talk after dark.

"Take her directly home, say good night to her under the porch light, and get out of Dodge. If you go to the park, don't get over behind that big sycamore tree. You know they call that Lover's Lair for a reason."

Exactly where he'd taken her. At least they'd read the Bible together there.

Ryler swallowed. "I feel like a teenager."

"Women can make you feel that way." Grayson steepled his fingertips. "Besides the physical, how do you feel about Shell? Do you care about her?"

A boulder lodged in his throat. "I love her."

"How does she feel about you?"

"I'm not sure. Sometimes I think she cares. It's almost like she's scared to really feel. Afraid she'll get hurt or something."

"If you love her, show her you're not going anywhere. Show her she can trust you. You have a commitment to God to treat her with respect and honor her. Let God give you the strength."

"I was hoping for an easy solution, like a chastity belt or something."

Grayson laughed. "If you try everything and you're still tempted then marry her."

"I'd love to, but I'm not sure I can get her to agree."

"In God's sight, you're already married."

"Huh?"

"You became one flesh."

"But I've—um—in that case, I've married a lot of women." Heat warmed Ryler's neck. "But I've never been legally married."

"And you can't make it right with all of them."

"Shell's the only woman I've ever loved."

"Then do right by her."

"I will."

"And save the staircase thing for your honeymoon, but don't throw her over your shoulder. Women don't like to be hauled. Go Clark Gable. Only, less forceful."

❧

The drive to Shell's had been mostly silent, as if they both had so much on their minds they couldn't think of anything to say. He'd walked her to her door, but there'd been no physical contact and she'd scurried inside with a mumbled good night.

Ryler pulled into his driveway, his headlights illuminating a figure sitting on the porch steps.

Collin.

He killed the engine and stepped out of the SUV.

"Hey. I was hoping we could talk."

"About?"

"All this time, you knew. We're brothers. Why didn't you say anything?"

"I wanted to get to know you first." Ryler shrugged. "And I wasn't sure if you and Laken even knew about me. I didn't want to show up and blow your worlds apart." Been there.

"Admit it, you were scared of Mother."

Ryler chuckled. "She was kind of scary when I worked for her, and I'll admit at one point, I wanted to fade away, but I couldn't. Knowing I had a brother and sister, I couldn't just leave."

"I'm glad. I think, maybe this family can really be a family. For the first time." Collin ran a hand through his hair.

"Growing up, I never measured up for Father. He was really tough on me."

"And Laken?"

"He ignored her."

Ryler frowned. Maybe he didn't want to get to know Martin Kroft after all.

"I know now, he was hurting. He could never look past the son he'd lost to see the son and daughter he had."

"I'm sorry."

"It's not your fault."

"It's not yours either."

"You're right." Collin stood. "I better get home. I promised I'd call Jill and tell her how it went with us."

Ryler's gaze narrowed. "She made you come over here."

"Jill doesn't make me do anything." Collin grinned. "Other than follow her around like a lovesick puppy. No, I came because I wanted to. I'm calling her because our semblance of a family blows her mind and she's worried about me."

Must be nice to have someone worry.

"Don't let what I said about Father scare you off." Collin offered his hand. "With you in the equation, maybe we can all heal. Together."

Hmm. Shake, hug, or just say *See ya*.

Collin hugged him and they clapped each other on the back.

Despite the manly stiffness of the embrace, Ryler's eyes filled with tears. Thank goodness it was dark and the porch light was burned out.

Pulling away, Collin gave him a final *thud* on the back and jogged across the street.

&

Chair legs scraped against the tiled floor of the Rambler Café then quieted as the lunch crowd headed back to work. Shell's stomach fluttered, partly because of Ryler's nearness and partly from anxiety over the expected phone call.

Today was the day. The day they'd learn once and for all that Ryler was officially a Kroft. Officially out of her league.

Trying to concentrate on something other than him, she

stared out the front window as numerous cars and pickup trucks pulled away.

The waitress brought strawberry cheesecake on one dish with a plump berry resting beside the generous slice.

"Could we have another plate?" Shell asked.

"This is fine." Ryler winked at her.

Her heart swooned.

"If I was twenty years younger, honey"—the waitress propped a hand on her hip—"I'd eat from the same dish with him."

Ryler's eyes widened as the waitress left them alone.

Shell stifled a giggle.

"What? You think I've got germs or something?"

"We're sitting on the same side of the table. If we eat out of the same dish, it becomes—"

"An official date. You okay with that?"

She wanted to be. If he wasn't a Kroft. If he could just stay Ryler Grant. "What did you and Grayson talk about last night?"

He blushed. Ryler Grant blushed. Or Martin Rothwell Kroft? Or whoever he was.

"Guy stuff. What did you and Adrea talk about?"

"Just girl stuff." She scooped up a bite of the cheesecake dripping with sauce.

Gently, he picked up the fruit by the cap. "Wait, do you want the strawberry?"

"Sure."

He held it in front of her mouth.

Her breath caught. "I can feed myself."

"Humor me."

As she bit the strawberry in two, his gaze stayed on her lips. Self-consciously, she chewed and swallowed. "I've never done anything so cheesy in my life."

"It may have been cheesy, but I really shouldn't have done that."

"Why?"

" 'Cause it made me want to kiss you, and we're in a public place."

She looked down and popped the bite of dessert dripping from her spoon into her mouth.

"Now you've got whipped cream on your lip, which makes me want to kiss you even more."

His cell vibrated.

Her gaze flew to his. "Answer it."

With trembling fingers, he slid the phone open. "Hello?"

Her heart launched into double-time as she watched his expression.

He swallowed hard. "We'll be right over."

"Sylvie? What did she say?"

eight

"She said my father wants to meet me." Ryler's voice cracked.

Her stomach took a nosedive. *Don't let any disappointment show. Be happy for him.*

Wrapping her arms around his shoulders, she hugged him, even though the news sealed their fate. "Oh, Ryler, I knew it, but it's nice to officially know it."

"Tell me about it."

"I can't go with you."

"You have to."

"You're meeting your father for the first time. You do not need me tagging along."

"I need all the moral support I can get. Please come. You can wait outside or in another room, but I need you there."

He needed her.

Her heart tumbled.

He didn't need her. He needed some debutante with blue blood to match his.

But for today, she'd be there for him. And tomorrow. She wouldn't think about tomorrow just yet.

She grabbed the bill and took his hand. "Let's go. We'll stop by the B & B and get my car in case you want to stay for a while."

❧

Ryler gulped a deep breath, his hand hovering over the doorbell.

"It'll be fine." Shell rubbed her hand over his back. "You're about to meet a man who's longed to see you your entire life. He loves you."

"What if he's drunk?"

"I'm sure you've seen a few drunks in your life."

He paced away from the door, leaning one hand on the

column of the porch. "What if he's angry that I didn't come forward sooner?"

"Relax." She hooked her hand through his elbow and propelled him back to the door. "Take another deep breath and ring the bell. Am I going to have to do it for you again?"

His finger moved toward the button but the door opened.

Sylvie greeted him with a tremulous smile and a hug. "I'm so glad you're here."

What to call her? Sylvie didn't sound right, but neither did Mom. Laken and Collin called her Mother. Mother? An outsider in his own family.

"Your father's waiting in the den. He hasn't had anything to drink today."

"Did you tell him I was coming?"

"No. I told him Laken and Collin were and he knows they'll only come if he doesn't drink."

Shell pushed him toward the double doors.

"You expect me to walk in and drop my bomb with no warning."

"Son, he's waited for this bomb for thirty years."

"Go on." Shell kissed his cheek. "I'll be here when you get back. Don't make him wait any longer."

Ryler sucked in another deep breath and strode toward the den.

"Shell, everyone else is in the family room, if you'd like to join them. Once Martin and Ryler have had some time together, we'll see you there."

Needing extra strength, he turned to face her.

She flashed him a brave smile.

Ryler pulled the double doors open.

Martin Kroft sat on the white sofa. Tall and thin, with stooped shoulders and shaky hands. Yellow-white hair, sallow skin, dark circles sank under dim blue eyes.

"Do I know you, young man?"

"Not yet, sir."

"You remind me of someone." He shook a finger at Ryler then pressed a trembly hand against his lips. "My father. You remind me of my father when he was young. The spitting image. Sylvie?"

"Martin"—with a quiver in her voice, Sylvie took Ryler's arm and propelled him forward—"this is our son."

The older man's eyes widened and a sob escaped him. "How did you find. . . ?" He threw his arms open wide.

Ryler didn't need another father. He already had one. But somehow he felt drawn to the beckoning arms.

He sat beside Martin Kroft on the couch and quivery arms encircled him. Sobs echoed in his ears and pressure welled inside his chest. A low moan escaped him as Sylvie wrapped her arms around them both, her tears soaking into Ryler's shoulder.

"You're home. My boy is home. I'm so sorry. I didn't want you to see me like this."

❧

The double doors opened and Shell jumped up, clasping her hands in front of her, then behind her.

Ryler came out first. His red-rimmed eyes tore at her.

"Thanks for waiting." He reached for her hand.

Sylvie latched on to his other arm as if he might get away. "You okay?"

"Sylvie, can you give us a minute? I promise I won't leave."

Sylvie let go of him. "I guess I really should see about Martin. It's been an emotional afternoon. Especially for him. You two talk here and maybe when he's ready, we can all join the others together."

"You okay?" Shell repeated as the double doors closed.

"I think so. He cried like a baby, so I did, too."

She cupped his cheek. "How is he?"

"He's a shell of what he should be. The drinking has taken a toll on him."

"Maybe having you here will give him incentive to get help."

"Maybe. I can't tell you how much I appreciate you being here." He brushed a soft kiss across her lips and pulled her into his arms.

The double doors opened and they jerked away from each other.

"Well, who do we have here?" an unfamiliar voice asked.

Martin Kroft had all of Ryler's height, but none of the muscle. Rail thin, with sickly yellow skin and faded blue eyes. But he'd once been a handsome man.

"This is Shell Evans."

"Your lady?"

Ryler grinned. "I'd like her to be. Right now, just call us friends, for her peace of mind."

"Nice to meet you, Shell." He extended a shaky hand toward her.

He needed a drink. Bad. "Nice to meet you, sir."

"Through here." Sylvie led the way.

Two taupe couches and several chairs furnished the large family room. A huge TV dwarfed the central wall. Soft gold walls, hardwood floors with a glossy sheen, and a large area rug with splashes of red gave the room a cozy feel despite its size.

Jill hovered near Collin, as if she felt as out of place as Shell did. The total-honesty policy must include news of new brothers.

"Ryler, welcome to the family." Hayden offered his hand. "Sorry about all that other stuff."

"So, now that we have proof"—Laken frowned—"will Ryler still have to petition the court to open his adoption records?"

"Why?" Ryler shrugged.

"To claim your trust fund, of course." Collin took a sip of his tea.

Trust fund? Ryler had never said anything about a trust fund.

"Ahem." Hayden coughed. "Do we need to get into this now?"

"Shell and Jill are close enough to family." Laken covered her mouth with one hand. "I do hope Collin told you about his trust fund, Jill."

"He did." Jill threaded her fingers through Collin's. "He's

learning about not keeping secrets."

Apparently, Ryler hadn't.

"I couldn't ask her to marry me without telling her about the trust fund." Collin squeezed Jill's hand. "Might as well reveal our warts and all, so she'll know what she's getting into."

"I didn't come here for money." Ryler's fists clenched.

Laken touched his arm. "That's not what I meant."

"No one thinks you're here for money, son." Sylvie latched on to his arm again. "You could have petitioned the court and claimed your inheritance without contacting us. But you must claim it. Your father and I want you to have the money."

But if Shell kept hanging around, everyone would think she only wanted the money.

"What if I don't claim it?"

Martin shrugged. "I guess if you don't, it'll eventually go to the state. But it's your money, son."

"Number one, money's never been important to me. Number two, if I claim the money, I feel like it will always cause doubts. Someone will always wonder if that's all I came for."

"Only if you take the money and run." Martin took a glass Laken offered. With his trembling, he almost dropped it. He drained it and set it on the coffee table.

"And Ryler wouldn't do that." Sylvie patted his arm.

"If I leave Romance, I won't take a dime with me."

"See. But you won't be leaving Rose Bud, son. Unless you want to move to Searcy. Your father and I couldn't bear to lose you again."

"Listen, I don't know what my plans are right now. It's been a long day, so I think Shell and I should be going. We both have an early day tomorrow."

"Can you have supper with us tomorrow night? Just Martin and me?" Anxiety shone in Sylvie's eyes.

"Probably." He patted her arm. "I'm not going anywhere. I'll call you."

Sylvie nibbled on the inside of her lip and gave a slight nod.

Martin hugged him again.

He ushered Shell through the house and headed to their separate vehicles.

"I wish we'd ridden together."

"I thought you might want to stay longer and you probably should." Hurt and disappointment warred within her. "It's kind of sweet the way Sylvie clings to you."

"And suffocating." He opened her car door for her.

"She's got a lifetime to make up for." She positioned the door between them. "So, did you plan to tell me about the trust fund?"

"Eventually." He grinned. "I'm still getting used to the idea of it."

"Your family doesn't approve of me."

"Why would you think that?"

"They think I'm a gold digger, just like my mother."

"They probably don't even know your mother." His lips brushed hers. "Sylvie loves you. I love you, Shell."

Tears burned her eyes. Words she'd never heard before. Words she could get used to. But could he really love "trailer trash", as the kids in school had called her? Until her mother had found rich men to upgrade their living status.

"Trust me, everyone in Searcy knows my mother and her penchant for taking up with rich men and milking all she could from them. It was only after her youth faded that she turned to prostitution and drugs."

"You don't seem to be hurting for money, Shell." He gestured toward her vehicle. "You drive a nice, late-model sports car, you've worked for Darrell for years, and I imagine he pays you well for your expertise. Why would anyone worry about you wanting my trust fund? I haven't even claimed it yet, and I'm not sure I will."

"I just think you should have told me about it." Sarcasm dripped from her tone as she settled in her car and fastened the seat belt. "Since you love me and all."

"Maybe"—his teeth clenched—"I need you to admit you love me back before I'm willing to share everything with you."

She started the engine and gunned it. That was something

she wasn't willing to admit. If she admitted she loved him, then she'd have to try to keep up with the Joneses. And she'd learned long ago, she couldn't. Shell Evans wasn't of the same ilk.

❧

The phone rang for the eighth time. Pacing his kitchen, Ryler ran his hand through his hair. No cool ringtone. No-nonsense ringing, like Shell. *Come on, pick up.*

Would she even answer? He didn't like the way she'd left.

Finally, he'd blurted out his feelings for her. But she hadn't returned the sentiment.

"Hello?"

"Shell, I'm so glad I caught you. Are you going to Conway this weekend?"

"I'm packing now."

"Will you be back for church Sunday?"

"I was planning to go with Savannah there. Why?"

"Laken called to make sure I'd be at church Sunday. Martin's coming."

Her gasp echoed over the handset. "Wow."

"Tell me about it. Laken said he hasn't gone since she was eleven." He paced into the living room. "I was hoping you'd be there."

"I'll come back Saturday night."

"Good. I feel a lot more comfortable with you than I do with them."

"You're one of them, Ryler. Let that sink into your stubborn brain."

"I'm trying. Thanks, Shell. Sorry to cut your time with Chance short."

"It's okay. Three more weeks and I'll be back home with him anyway."

Three weeks. Only three more weeks of working with her, seeing her daily. He couldn't let her leave him. Not again.

"I'll see you Sunday then. Safe trip." He wanted to say he loved her, but he didn't want to scare her any further away.

At least she didn't sound mad. But distant. As if, in her mind, she was already gone.

He'd just have to change her mind.

Something clattered at the front door. Another clatter.

Ryler frowned and hurried to open the door.

Brady sat beside the porch, with a basketball in his lap and a crushed aluminum can poised in his fist. "Hey."

"Hey." Ryler's chest felt all fuzzy.

"Dad says you're my uncle."

"It's true."

"I thought we might play some basketball, if you have time."

Ryler nodded. "You're on."

"I'm playing basketball with Uncle Ryler," Brady called.

Uncle Ryler. His heart warmed. He glanced across the road.

Collin waved then went inside.

"So, Dad says you just found out about us." Brady swished the ball through the hoop.

Ryler jogged to rebound. "A few months back."

"I think Dad wishes you'd grown up with him and Aunt Laken."

"What gives you that idea?" Ryler lobbed the ball back to Brady.

"I heard him talking to Aunt Laken on the phone, about how everything would have been different if they'd found you sooner. Kind of like if my dad had learned about me sooner."

"I guess so."

"Sometimes I wonder if I'd have always lived with Dad, would I be able to walk?" Brady swallowed hard. "When I was little, I ran out and tried to get in the truck to go to work with Hayden and he backed into me."

Ryler stifled a gasp.

"That probably wouldn't have happened if I'd lived with Dad. But then I think about how God's got it all worked out and we just have to trust Him." Brady swished the ball through the hoop again.

"If I'd lived with Dad, he might have been so sad over

Mom, he couldn't have taken care of me good. I might have wandered into the road and died. Then he'd have felt guilty and maybe he couldn't have dealt with guilt the way Hayden has. Maybe if you'd always lived with Mimi and Poppa, your other parents would have been really sad and lonely. And maybe Poppa would've still started drinking, but he wouldn't have ever had a reason to stop."

"How'd you get so smart?"

"I heard Pastor Grayson preach about it once. He said when bad things happen, that God might be saving us from something worse. Like maybe his first wife died the way she did because she was going to get cancer or something and suffer a lot. I thought it made sense."

"It makes a lot of sense." Maybe Shell hadn't been together enough to raise Chance. Maybe some jerk she'd dated would have mistreated her innocent son. Maybe Shell had done the best thing she could at the time.

&

Martin Kroft Sr. had kept his promise. Sunday morning, Shell sat surrounded by Ryler's entire family.

Outnumbered and outclassed.

As Grayson finished his sermon, the music began.

Ryler, Laken, and Collin went to the altar first. In a huddle, they knelt as Shell dabbed at her eyes. Sylvie stepped into the aisle and Martin followed her. Brady rolled himself down the aisle, as well. A few others knelt.

As the song wound down, only the Krofts were still at the altar, with Grayson and Martin whispering back and forth. They all stood and faced the congregation.

Collin crooked his finger at Jill, who joined him and Hayden went up to stand with Laken. Ryler gestured to Shell.

Me? You want me up there with you? She shook her head, quick and sharp.

He gestured again.

Shell rolled her eyes and went to stand with him.

His arm came around her waist.

"The Krofts have a new family member they'd like you to meet." When he finished speaking, Grayson sat in one of the chairs on the stage.

Sylvie stepped to the microphone. "Several months ago, I asked everyone to pray for Martin and me to find our oldest son. Your prayers worked." Sylvie's voice quivered as she took Ryler's hand. "This is our son, Ryler Grant."

Excited gasps and whispers moved through the crowd.

Martin Sr. stepped up beside them. "Hello, everyone, I'm Martin Kroft, and I'm an alcoholic."

Tears coursed down Sylvie's cheeks and Laken hugged her father.

Shell wiped her eyes with the back of her hand.

"All these years I've drank to get over losing our son, and in the process, I lost the two children I already had. I'm sorry." Martin's watery gaze locked on Collin. "I want to stop. I want to live. I want to get to know my kids. All of them."

Collin moved closer and put his arm around Martin's shoulders.

Sniffles from the crowd filled the silence. Shell scanned the faces. Not a dry eye in the house, except for a few oblivious children.

"Please pray for me." Martin started back to his pew, flanked by his family.

Shell bypassed the pew and went straight to the ladies' room. Staring in the mirror, she imagined how out of place she'd been up there. Laken with inner kindness shining from her eyes. Collin, a work in progress, but changing. Sylvie, a new creature—and Martin on the verge of a new life. Yet, even after all the years Martin and Sylvie had been together, he obviously didn't fit.

Laken, Collin, Sylvie. They were all flawed, but their purebred class oozed from every pore. All that oozed from Shell was wrong-side-of-the-tracks mutt.

The door opened and an older woman with hair too dark for her age came in and offered her hand. "Oh, I wanted to meet you, Shelly. I've heard so much about you. I'm Doreen

Hughes." Black penciled eyebrows scrunched together and her entire face puckered like she'd sucked on a lemon. "Am I to understand you're dating Sylvie's son?"

"We're just friends. And my name is Shell, not Shelly. Excuse me." Shell hurried out, managed to sidestep the straggling crowd, and fled outside to freedom.

~

Ryler jogged to catch up with her. Though Shell had a good head start, her heels slowed her progress. "Shell."

Halfway down the long drive of the B & B, she stopped. With a big sigh, she turned to face him.

"What?"

"You okay?"

"Fine."

"We're all going to lunch at the folks' house in Searcy. Want to come?"

"No, you go with your family."

"I feel kind of out of place with them."

"Trust me, you're not. You fit right in. It's in your blood."

"I was hoping you'd come with me."

"You don't need me tagging along, Ryler. Just go. Have a good time with your family. I'm going to Conway to spend the rest of the day with Chance, anyway."

"When do I get to meet him?"

"You don't." There was something final in her eyes.

"You're coming back, aren't you?"

"This place isn't finished, is it?" Sarcasm tinged her voice as she gestured toward the mess in the front yard. "I think I'll spend the night, though, and come back early in the morning."

"Are we okay?"

"We, as in. . . ?"

"We, as in us. I'm trying to build a relationship with you, Shell."

"We've got a lot going on right now." Her eyes were too shiny. "You're getting to know a whole new family. And I—I just want to get home to Chance. Besides, I've got a grand opening bash to plan.

"In two weeks this job will be done. Until then, I can't think about much else. Let's see how it goes then. Maybe absence won't make the heart grow fonder."

"So you're basically saying you don't want to see me."

She rolled her eyes. "I'm saying, you need to spend time with your newfound family and I need to spend time with my son and party planning. That doesn't leave much time for anything else."

"I'll make time."

"Not now, Ryler. Let's concentrate on getting this job finished." She turned away and ran toward her apartment.

Finish the job so she could walk out of his life again. He couldn't let her do it.

૨ઠ

Ryler mentally patted himself on the back for giving his helper the day off with only a week left before the grand opening. He snuck a glance at Shell crawling around on her hands and knees, with dirt on her nose, looking way too cute.

With a grin, he flipped a trowel of dirt on her back.

Shell stiffened then turned and flung a fistful in his face.

Retaliation came as he smeared another handful down her shoulder.

Her world-weary sigh grated on his nerves.

"Ryler, please. We've got work to do."

He tackled her and rolled her over, poised with a handful over her mouth.

Blue eyes pleaded. "We need to finish this job."

He dropped the dirt on the ground. "You've got something on your nose." As he wiped the smear away, more than anything, he wanted to kiss her. His gaze locked on her lips.

nine

"Good thing the workers are all inside." Pushing away from him, she hurried to put some distance between them. "Truce."

Her rejection sliced through him.

"Except this nice, plump earthworm would look great in your hair."

She screamed, jumped up, and ran.

"I was kidding."

"Well, it's not funny."

"You're afraid of earthworms."

"Not really afraid of them. They're just so"—she shivered—"so yucky."

He laughed and shoved the worm in her direction again.

Though she was ten feet away from him, she did a heebie-jeebie dance. "Stop it."

"Ryler, really." Sylvie's tone reprimanded. "Stop torturing the poor girl."

His mother stood with Helen Fenwick.

What to call her? Mother? Mom? "Afternoon, Sylvie."

Shell's eyes widened.

"I'm sure you remember Helen. Helen, my son Ryler."

"Nice to meet you, ma'am. I'd offer a handshake, but. . ." Ryler swiped his hands together.

"I was at the floral shop, where Helen works part-time, this morning. Adrea sent her over to discuss the arrangements for the grand opening and I thought I'd join her to see how things were coming here." Sylvie looked as if she might pounce on him with a hug, despite the grime.

"I can't." Shell rubbed shaky hands down her thighs. "Ryler's helper isn't here today, so I have to help him. And besides, I'm a mess."

"Heavens, Ryler, what did you do, roll her in the dirt?"

He winked at Shell. "I can spare you for a bit." But not for long. Too long and he'd miss her. But he knew she needed to make peace with Helen.

With a hard swallow, Shell clapped her hands together. "Maybe, if Helen can excuse my appearance, I could spare an hour or so."

"Oh, it won't take nearly that long, dear, and a little dirt never hurt anything. Adrea wanted me to check each room's size, so we can scale the arrangements to fit."

❧

Tough choice. Shell ground her back teeth together. Deal with Ryler or Wade's mother?

"I'll stay here and keep Ryler company." Sylvie perched on a white iron bench, well away from the dirt.

Great. Alone with Wade's mother. Shell wasn't sure she'd made the right decision as she led Helen to the house.

"There are a lot of stairs." Shell slowed her pace to match Helen's. "Are you sure you'll be all right?"

"I'm fine." Helen leaned into her cane with each step. "The exercise will be good for me. You know, I never had a bit of trouble with arthritis until I broke this hip."

Did Helen know she'd gotten pregnant? Did she think there had been an abortion? A miscarriage? Whatever Helen thought, Chance's grandmother was oblivious to his existence.

"Thank you for coming to the funeral."

Shell's breath caught. "You seem okay."

"I lean on Jesus and I have peace about where Wade is." Helen grasped Shell's arm as they stepped inside the house.

"When did Wade become a Christian?"

"About the time he went into rehab and then had that long stretch of sobriety."

They stopped in the living room. "Oh my, Shell, you've done wonders with this place. It's lovely."

"Thank you." A sense of accomplishment put a real smile on her face.

"I know what you're thinking."

"You do?"

"You're wondering how I can believe Wade is in heaven after all the bad things he did."

"Well—"

"God says, 'I will never leave thee, nor forsake thee.' That's in Hebrews 13:5. We might turn our backs on Him, but He's faithful. And besides, in the end, Wade made peace with God. I can't tell you how I've clung to that. He was drunk and not in his right mind when he. . ."

"I'm glad you're okay. You've been through a lot."

"Sometimes, I feel alone, but God reminds me I've got Him, my church, and countless friends."

And a grandson you don't know about.

Helen squeezed her arm. "I'm excited about the grand opening. This project will be so much fun."

Shell's heart twisted with a mix of emotions. After the grand opening, Shell would go home. Home to Chance. Away from Ryler. For good.

&

Ryler took his ball cap off and threw it onto his truck seat. Scrubbing his hand over his curls, he tried to erase the ring of flattened hair around his head a full day of work caused. No use, he plopped the hat back on. He probably should wait and stop by the RoZark Hills Roasterie before work in the morning, but his cupboard was bare. No coffee. He couldn't go home without it. And he'd already placed his order earlier in the day.

He pulled in and parked next to a familiar dark maroon Cadillac. Darrell hadn't mentioned he'd be in town today. Climbing out of his truck, he glanced down at his dirt-and-grass-streaked jeans. His work boots were caked in mud. They might not let him in. He stomped both feet and tried to dust some of the grime from his clothing.

Surely they'd forgive a guy suffering from coffee withdrawals for stopping in straight from work.

The bell jingled above the door as he opened it. He closed

his eyes and inhaled the coffee aroma, almost tasting a savory cup in the air.

The owner was talking to someone, so Ryler went to the shelf with his favorite chocolate-covered coffee beans. Five of these babies and the top of his head buzzed. He picked his favorite, white chocolate.

"Now, our Blueberry Cobbler blend would be a nice morning coffee for your guests."

"Oh, that sounds heavenly."

Shell's voice.

Ryler stiffened.

Peering around the silver shelf loaded with fancy coffee cups and pots, he spotted her. With Darrell. Standing too close to her.

He could quietly back out the door, but the bell would ring and she'd probably already seen him.

"Once the B & B opens, Shell will have full authority to try new blends, but I'd like something more—"

"Darrell means the new manager he's going to hire *any day now* will have full authority. I won't be here."

Darrell spotted him and rolled his eyes. "Don't you think we need something more manly for the B & B? Would you want blueberry cobbler coffee?"

Ryler cleared his throat. "I'm a Columbian kind of guy, myself."

"We have your order ready. One pound of Columbian La Ladera. I'll be right with you."

"Now, that sounds like coffee." Darrell surveyed the list of flavors.

"That would be a nice evening coffee. Not too heavy, but rich flavor with a hint of caramel," the wife half of the owner team said as she grinned at Ryler. "The new B & B is going to serve our coffee."

"They won't regret it. Best coffee in the state."

"Did you know her husband set up the first Starbucks factory in New York?" Darrell touched Shell's elbow.

Ryler's breath stalled. "I'll come back. I'm kind of

embarrassed coming in here looking like this anyway."

"Oh, you're fine." The owner waved a carefree hand at him.

"Here, ring him up real quick." Darrell stepped aside, linking his arm with Shell's. "No sense in you coming back."

Shell never even looked at him as Ryler handed the owner a ten and a five and grabbed his treats. "Keep the change."

"You sure? Don't you want a bag?"

"No, I'm fine. Thanks." Ryler rushed out and jumped into his truck.

So why was she with Darrell? And why wasn't Darrell's wife with him? Why did it require Shell *and* Darrell to choose coffee for the B & B?

❧

Finally, the grand opening.

Standing on her haven, the balcony, Shell took deep breaths.

The orchestra played from the pristine lawn in front of the miniature Romance Waterfalls. The stringed instruments, backed by trickling water, soothed her frayed nerves.

All evening, she'd avoided Ryler. Since Darrell still hadn't hired a manager, she'd tag-teamed with Eva as they'd answered question after question, given tour after tour, and greeted guest after guest.

She'd even given tours of the apartment. Officially the honeymoon suite now, as all of her things were already packed.

The soft breeze ruffled the sheer overlay of her pale blue dress. Since many on the guest list were from Searcy, countless wide-eyed guests had stared at her, as if they didn't know she could clean up so well. As if they couldn't imagine Wade Fenwick's floozy had achieved such an accomplishment as the immaculate Rose Bud Bed & Breakfast.

"There you are." Darrell's voice came from behind her.

She turned to face him and smiled at an older, well-to-do couple beside him.

"Mr. and Mrs. Morris Vanderhaven, meet Shell Evans, the mastermind behind this renovation project."

Shell's mouth went dry. The last time she'd seen Mr. Vanderhaven, she was fifteen and he'd been in her mother's bed.

Now, he looked as if he might pass out.

"The Vanderhavens live in Searcy, and Morris is the president of Home Town Bank."

Might as well put the old philanderer's mind at ease.

Shell mustered up a smile and offered her hand. "So nice to meet you both."

"This place is absolutely gorgeous." Mrs. Vanderhaven's natural Southern belle drawl warmed Shell's heart.

Such a sweet lady didn't deserve an unfaithful husband.

"Morris, I'd love to spend our next anniversary here."

Mr. Vanderhaven cleared his throat. "Well, um, we'll see."

"I wish I could stay here, too." Shell clutched the railing. "But the renovation project is finished, so I'll be going back to the apartments I manage in Conway."

Mr. Vanderhaven visibly relaxed. "Perhaps we could make arrangements to stay here."

"The clerks are already in the lobby taking reservations."

"Oh, let's hurry." Mrs. Vanderhaven led her anxious husband through the door. "I want one of these two rooms close to the balcony."

"I'll be right there." Darrell's eyebrows drew together. "What was that about?"

"Trust me, you don't want to know."

"You okay?" He put a brotherly arm around her shoulders.

"A little worse for wear."

A series of loud pops made her jump. Fireworks of every color streaked through the sky.

"We should have put this shindig off another two weeks and scheduled it for the Fourth of July."

"I couldn't take another two weeks, and besides, it's on a Thursday this year. We couldn't have a grand opening on a Thursday."

"You made this place what I always knew it could be, and tomorrow you can go home to Chance." He gave her arm a squeeze. "I sure wish my wonderful wife didn't have to commute back and forth to run this place."

Shell sighed. "You're not guilting me into staying. All you have to do is hire someone."

"None of the applicants were right, since the perfect manager refused to apply," he said pointedly. "I better go make sure Mrs. Vanderhaven gets the exact room she wants. You coming? I still need you to help Eva work the crowd."

"In a minute." Closing her eyes, Shell inhaled the honeysuckle scent of the evening air as Darrell's footsteps faded away.

"Shell Evans." A male voice sliced through her peace.

She turned around.

Pete Callaway stood in the doorway. Pete Callaway, her first crush. The pimple-faced senior who'd taken her virginity during her sophomore year, then tossed her aside for his next conquest a few months later. The pimples were gone, but he was still gangly, all legs, and painfully thin.

"Hi, Pete." Nary a quiver in her voice. She mentally patted herself on the back.

"I couldn't believe my eyes when I looked up here and saw you standing at the railing. You look great. Really great." His gaze wandered slowly over every inch of her. "I haven't seen you since you were dating Wade."

She bit down the bitter revulsion threatening to rise up in her throat. What had she ever seen in him?

"I guess you don't live around here." She stepped back toward the railing. "Everyone knew I was here within a week of my arrival."

"I'm still in Romance. My numerous rental properties keep me really busy." His chest puffed up as he spoke.

Two old houses. Guess that was numerous to him. "Well, I better get back to my guests." She tried to slip past him.

He grabbed her wrist. "Now don't run off just yet. Maybe we could have coffee. Or *something*."

Forcing herself not to cringe, she smiled. "No thank you."

"We could get reacquainted, if you know what I mean."

Alcohol soured his breath, even though Grace was only serving tea and coffee.

"I know exactly what you mean." She tried to pull her wrist away, but he held fast. "And I'm not interested."

"Oh come on, Shell. The apple doesn't fall far from the tree."

Despite his painful grip, she managed to jerk her arm free.

"Keep your hands off her." Ryler's steely tone came from the doorway.

Pete whirled around. Both eyebrows rose. "Ryler Grant, isn't it? I was just welcoming Shell back to the area. Nice to see you here."

"Is it?"

"I better be getting back to the party." Pete slunk through the door.

She turned away from Ryler and worked at keeping her voice steady. "This turned into quite the bash. I was hoping for a hundred guests, but I think it's more like two. Good thing I ordered extra food."

Footsteps closed in on her. "You okay?" His voice came from just behind her.

"Fine."

He joined her at the railing. Tenderly, he caught her reddened wrist and inspected the marks. "I take it you know my landlord."

She sighed, not wanting to get into it, yet knowing Ryler wouldn't let it rest. "Remember the high school boyfriend Collin tried to steal me away from?"

"Pete?" He let go of her. "A real winner."

"The place looks great, doesn't it? We did a great job."

"We make a great team." His breath stirred the hair at the crown of her head.

She shivered.

"What now?"

"You find another job. I go back to Conway."

"But we make a great team."

She shrugged. "Who knows? We might work together again someday."

Gently gripping her shoulders, Ryler turned her to face him. "That's not what I meant, Shell. I want a future with you."

The brown pinstripe suit accentuated his broad shoulders and the moss-colored shirt mirrored his eyes. The evening breeze blew his dark chocolate waves.

Determination slipping, her gaze dropped to his chest. "My future is in Conway."

"Mine could be, too. I bet there's lots of landscaping jobs there."

"No. Your future is here—with your family."

"I love you, Shell." He tipped her chin up, until her gaze met his.

Wanting to press her cheek into his palm, her throat constricted. She swallowed hard, biting back the reciprocated words that threatened to tumble out. "It can't work. We're too different."

"You're more like me than anyone I've ever known. It's what initially drew me to you. We were both broken and used. Now we're Christians, healing and changing. Let's heal and change together."

"You're blue-blooded Kroft and I'm—"

"You're the most beautiful woman I've ever known, inside and out."

"My mother prostituted herself, Ryler."

"But that has nothing to do with who you are."

"Haven't you ever heard 'the apple doesn't fall far from the tree'? Even if I could forget my past, these high-class citizens can't. I see it in their eyes every time they look at me." She scanned the crowd below: Doreen Hughes, the Vanderhavens, and even Pete Callaway. She shuddered. *"Do you know who her mother is?"*

"You're imagining things."

She closed her eyes. "You saw Pete. You know what he wanted—what he expected—from me. I can't stay here and get away from that."

"Shell, stop it and listen to me. I want to marry you. I want us to raise Chance. Here or in Conway, wherever you want.

I want us to build a family together, maybe even have kids of our own someday."

"I'll never bring my son to this self-righteous town." *And I'll never let him down by telling him I'm his mother.*

"Shell," Darrell called.

Ryler's hands dropped to his sides.

She spotted her boss below the balcony. "I'll be right there."

"Sorry to interrupt, Ryler, but I need my right-hand gal down here."

"Maybe I was wrong about you." Ryler shook his head. "Maybe you are like your mother. Maybe you're shirking your responsibility. Maybe you're not raising your son so you can be free. Free to collect hearts you're unwilling to commit to."

"What's that supposed to mean?"

"From the moment I've known you, there's been only one constant in your life."

She shrugged, waiting for him to clue her in.

"Darrell. I saw him up here with you and whenever he beckons, you run to his side."

"I'm supposed to be working tonight." Shell bristled. "And Darrell is one of the finest men I've ever known."

"Oh yeah, then why is he cheating on his wife with you?" He turned away. "You don't care about anyone but yourself. At least my mother was forced to give me up."

Ryler stalked through the door.

On jelly legs, Shell scurried to the porch swing. Doubled over, she covered her face with both hands. Sobs shook her shoulders.

❧

Ryler stormed down the stairs and pushed through the crowd.

He'd seen Darrell up there with her, his arm around her. How could he have been so stupid? Obviously, it had been Darrell all along. Shell didn't want a commitment and Darrell couldn't commit. They were perfect for each other.

Shell was a Christian now, but she didn't have a clue about

right and wrong. Maybe she was one of those Grayson spoke about. Maybe she thought the rules didn't apply to her. Maybe she'd just been playing him and hadn't accepted Christ at all.

"Ryler," Pastor Grayson called. "This is Doreen Hughes. She was just asking me who did the landscaping."

His gaze rested on the multitude of roses in the garden surrounding the Romance waterfall replica, but the beauty failed to soothe the turmoil roiling within him.

"I'm sorry, I'm not feeling well." Ignoring the older woman, he headed for his SUV, jumped in, and started the engine. The car next to him had parked crooked. With a heavy sigh, he eased back and forth several times before he could safely get out of the slot. Finally free, he stomped the gas and roared down the long drive, spinning gravel as he careened onto the highway.

ten

Shell toured the house one last time. Her eyes, still puffy from last night's sobs, felt as heavy as her heart. A small reservation desk had been situated in part of the entry. The wood floors and plank walls gleamed.

Opening the door to the restroom behind the desk, she scanned the flawless tile surrounding the antique commode and pedestal sink. The downstairs bedroom was all done in sage and cream with shimmery, satin curtains. Plenty of closet space left beside the new bathroom.

Cutting through the entry, she stepped into the living room and ran her hand over the wall. Smooth as glass. The antique camelback couch, wingback chairs, and a gold chaise lounge facing the ancient fireplace, with the soot marks gone.

Thick tapestry curtains in gold, sage, and red paisley graced each window in the room. The wainscot in the kitchen and dining room was a pristine white. Billowy, lacy white curtains provided the bay window a bit of privacy, but still let plenty of light in. New antique-look fixtures gave the kitchen a cozy feel.

The narrow staircase up to the former servants' quarters hadn't been widened, but the steps had been, making the climb a bit easier. Both rooms done in gold and red had a rich, royal feel to them. The new bathroom was nice and roomy, still leaving plenty of closet.

She descended the stairs and retraced her path to the main staircase. The paneling in the upstairs landing had been removed and the nail holes painstakingly filled. The stairway up to the attic had been widened. This bedroom was her favorite. All done in cream and gold with velvet curtains, tasseled tiebacks, and molded valances. The iron bed frame was burnished umber with streaks of gold in the metal.

The bedroom on the left of the landing was red and cream with moiré curtains and swag valances. The bedroom on the right used the same fabrics in terra cotta and cream. Each bathroom continued the soothing color combination of each distinct room decor.

Perfect. Though modern, the entire place looked as if she'd stepped back in time. She descended the stairs and stepped outside. Closing the door with a final *thud*, she turned the knob to make sure it locked.

Head held high, she strode to her car and started the engine. The waterfall painting tugged at her, but it held too many memories of Ryler. Better to leave it. Pulling out of the drive, she turned toward Conway for the final time.

Home to Chance. Away from Ryler. Tears rimmed her lashes as the miles multiplied behind her.

❧

Chance played at Shell's feet, surrounded by sturdy, plastic trucks, cars, and tractors. "Vroom, vroom." His chunky little fingers launched a hot rod sailing across the floor and into her foot. He giggled and did it again.

She should be happy. This is where she'd wanted to be for months. With Chance.

But at the price of Ryler.

How could he think such things of her? Her eyes stung and she blinked several times. She'd gotten saved when he had. And even before that, she'd done lots of things she wasn't proud of, but she'd never had anything to do with married men.

And the thing that bothered her most was what he'd said about Chance. Was she shirking her responsibility?

No, everything she'd done was for Chance's sake. On his hands and knees, he crawled in a rapid circle, vrooming his little car as fast as he could. Happy and healthy.

She'd done the right thing in giving him up. Hadn't she?

❧

Tempted to stay home, Ryler had forced himself to get ready and drive to church instead. He was getting baptized today. He should be filled with joy.

Stepping inside the sanctuary, he scanned the crowd. No Shell. He really hadn't expected her. But she was supposed to have gotten baptized, too. He swallowed the bitter disappointment rising in his throat.

The older woman from last night's party entered from the side door.

Concentrate on work. It was all he had. That and a new family. But work was familiar. He could lose himself in work.

He hurried to speak with the woman. "Ma'am?"

"Yes." She turned to face him.

"I'm sorry I couldn't speak with you last night." He offered his hand. "I'm Ryler Grant."

"I hope you're feeling better." The older woman smiled. "Do you have a card? I'm a friend of your mother's and I'd like to have some work done on my grounds."

Ryler dug in his pocket. "Sure. Give me a call."

"Thank you, I will." Mrs. Hughes stashed the card in her purse and moved on.

Pastor Grayson caught up with him. "You all ready to get baptized?"

"I am."

"Is Shell okay?"

His jaw clenched. "I have no clue."

"She called and said she wouldn't be getting baptized today."

Ryler closed his eyes. "I thought she might back out."

"How are things? Between you, I mean?"

"She's moving back to Conway."

"I thought y'all were working toward something permanent."

"I wanted to." Ryler's heart did a little jolt. "But obviously, she didn't. I think her old lifestyle's still got a grip on her."

"Just give her time. Some folks can't wait to start fresh when they get saved." Pastor Grayson clapped him on the back. "Some it takes a while. She'll be fine, as long as she stays in church."

Except that she'd already turned away and embraced a married man.

The harpist trilled a hymn, a hint that the morning devotion would begin soon.

A hand slid into his elbow and Sylvie's pricey perfume announced her presence. "There you are, dear."

"Son." Martin's tremors had eased. "Heard you're getting baptized this morning."

"Yes."

"I'm proud of you." Martin's watery eyes closed for a moment.

Ryler swallowed. "Right back at ya."

Linking her free arm with Martin's, Sylvie led them to the Kroft pew.

&

Shell jiggled her feet under the table as the Sunday school class began. The first she'd ever attended as an adult. Her mind strayed to Ryler. He was getting baptized today. And she was supposed to have joined him. But she wasn't worthy. Everywhere she turned, her past rose up to remind her of exactly who she was.

"Then Peter opened his mouth, and said, 'Of a truth I perceive that God is no respecter of persons.'" The women's teacher, a middle-aged woman with gray-streaked hair, looked up from her Bible. "We live in the age of grace. God's marvelous grace. He is no respecter of persons.

"That means if the murderer accepts Christ, he is no worse than the saved soul who told a little white lie. The redeemed adulterer is no worse than the Christian homeless man who stole a loaf of bread to feed his family. The woman with the alabaster jar, Mary Magdalene, and the woman at the well all had bad reputations, but Jesus accepted them all."

A lump lodged in Shell's throat. She wanted to ask who the women were, but she was probably the only one in the class who didn't know. Oh, if only she knew the Bible like everyone else seemed to. Even Ryler.

Ryler.

"Turn to John 8:1–11." Pages rustled together as class members flipped to the right chapter. At least Shell could find John in the Bible Savannah had bought her.

She followed the verses as the teacher read about the woman caught in adultery. "And Jesus said unto her, 'Neither do I condemn thee: go, and sin no more.'"

Jesus' words sank into Shell's soul.

The teacher continued. "If you accept Jesus Christ as your Savior, you are worthy. He counts you worthy. He forgives you and He can no longer see your sin. So, why do we keep looking back and holding on to it? The truth will set you free. Grab on to His truth, give Him your sins, and stop taking them back. Live the redeemed life He wants you to live."

I will. Starting now.

Shell bowed her head and silently prayed. *Thank You, Lord, for saving my soul. Forgive me for not believing You could make me new. Forgive me for all the things I've done and help me to forgive myself.*

Thank You for this child You've given me, Lord. Give me courage to do what's right by him. And thank You for placing Ryler in my life this second time. Please don't let it be too late for us. Help us to build a relationship with You in the center and help us to glorify You.

❧

Shell slowed the rocking chair as Chance grew heavier against her shoulder. The taupe walls, safari animal border, and curtains soothed her frayed nerves.

Humming "Amazing Grace" she inhaled his scent of baby shampoo. At eighteen months, he was getting too big to rock. Already, his legs were long enough she had to prop his feet up in each side of the chair to make sure they didn't get squished.

She hated to put him down, but she needed to speak to Savannah and Jake without Chance overhearing. He didn't stir as she gently laid him in his toddler bed.

Jake relaxed in his recliner with the sports section, while Savannah curled on the couch with her hand on the bulge of her stomach, reading an inspirational novel.

"Hey, y'all."

"Chance asleep?" Savannah put her book down.

She hugged herself. "I've been thinking."

Jake lowered the newspaper, his brows drawn together. "You want him back?"

Shell paced the room. "Darrell always planned for me to manage the B & B. I'm moving to Rose Bud and I'd like to take Chance with me, on frequent visits. There's a really good day care, right next door." Her words tumbled out. "And most of the time, he could probably hang out with me." Darrell would probably let her keep some toys for him and a crib there.

"So you want him back?" Savannah's chin trembled.

"I don't want to just jerk him away from the people he's known as Mommy and Daddy." Her words tumbled out. "I want to take it slow. Over the next few weeks, I'd like us to explain who his real mommy is." *We'll talk about Daddy when he's old enough to understand.* "If these frequent trips work out and he adjusts well, then I'd like him to live with me."

"All fine and good, but do you have to move to Rose Bud?" Jake wadded the paper and stashed it by his chair, lowering his feet to the floor.

"I guess this has something to do with Ryler?" Savannah sat upright and patted the seat beside her.

Shell's stomach knotted. She sank to the couch. "I'm hoping it does. He wants to marry me and I said no because—well, it's a long story."

"Savannah and I have always expected you to reclaim Chance." Jake's voice cracked. "We've loved him and raised him, knowing we might lose him."

"I'm sorry." Her gaze dropped to the floor. They'd been so good to her and in return, she'd broken their hearts. A weight settled on her shoulders, and she couldn't bring herself to look at Savannah sniffling beside her.

"Don't be. He should be with you. We've both always agreed on that, but we wanted to make sure you were stable and devoted to him."

"I am now."

"I know." Savannah squeezed her hand. "We're so proud of you."

"But it will be hard on y'all if it works out."

"Yes, but we knew that from the beginning." Savannah patted her stomach. "This baby won't replace Chance. We'll always love him as if he were our own."

"I know and I love you both for being there for him when I didn't feel able." Her gaze scanned the many family pictures lining the taupe walls. Pictures of Jake, Savannah, and Chance. Pictures of her, Savannah, and Chance. Pictures of just her with Chance. They'd painstakingly included her in the family unit.

"Who is this Ryler?" Jake asked.

"He's a Christian. He's a stable, good man from a good family."

"That's my only concern." Jake cleared his throat. "I don't want Chance jerked around. What if it doesn't work out with Ryler? And the reality of raising a child sets in and you don't feel up to the challenge?"

"Ryler's the one who convinced me Chance should be with me. He knows I'm a package deal. He wants to marry me and raise Chance."

But did he still want her? And if he really thought those awful things about her, did she want him?

She sucked in a deep breath, blinking away tears. "But don't worry, Jake. With or without Ryler, I want Chance with me and he'll be my first priority.

"Even if things don't work out with him"—her stomach did an odd tilt—"or if the reality of an eighteen-month-old is too much for him, then Chance and I will be fine without him." The words tasted bitter. "Either way, Chance comes first. The way he should have from the beginning."

"He's always come first." Savannah squeezed her hand again. "You were convinced that us raising him was better for him. It's not like you gave him up because you didn't want him."

Tears singed Shell's eyes. "You're right, and it was the hardest thing I've ever done."

"When do you plan on leaving?" Savannah's voice wobbled.

"Saturday morning, if it's okay with y'all and Chance. I've got some things to take care of here, like moving my stuff and talking with Darrell. And I want to ease Chance into this. There's no rush."

Except her heart longed for Ryler. Could they get past his absurd accusations about Darrell? Could they look toward the future, together?

"We'll try a couple of days to start with. I want him to meet a couple of people, but if he gets homesick, I'll bring him back early. I promise. The last thing I want is for my son to be miserable."

"Then, you have our blessing." Jake strode over and squeezed between them, hugging them both.

વ

Singsong jabber from the backseat warmed Shell's soul. Chance was a great little traveler.

Ryler's SUV was gone. Across the street, Collin's car was, too. Where could Ryler be? The trash cans that usually sat by the road were gone. With the curtains pulled shut, the house looked oddly abandoned. Surely he couldn't have cleared out in a week's time. *Lord, please don't let him have left town.*

For the next seven miles, she prayed.

Several cars were parked in the B & B lot. Business was booming.

An eighth of a mile farther, Hayden's truck sat in the drive of his and Laken's house, but her car was gone. All three siblings gone. Breakfast at the Krofts'.

Shell concentrated on the mailbox numbers. She had to introduce Chance to someone else first.

In the front yard of a neat house, Helen worked with a hoe in a flower garden. Turning, she shielded her eyes from the sun's glare and smiled as Shell got out. "Hello, what a nice surprise."

"I have someone with me I'd like you to meet." Shell ducked into the backseat and undid Chance's safety harness. His pale green short set, with dolphins swimming around the waist, was clean and adorable. Perfect for meeting his grandmother.

He giggled as she swooped him up in the air and propped him on her hip. She strode toward Helen.

"What a cutie." Helen tickled a bare foot.

Chance responded with a gurgly giggle.

"He had shoes on, but he loves taking them off."

"Let's go inside, so he can get down." Helen led the way to the house. "Goodness me, I don't have any toys. I don't usually get such young, handsome visitors."

"I have some in my bag, but maybe we'll keep some here in the future. I think Chance will be visiting often."

Helen frowned as they stepped inside. Obviously questions quivered on her lips, but manners kept her from asking.

Pictures of Wade stared at Shell from every wall and surface. She shivered, wishing she could go back and undo things. Yet, if she'd never stolen Wade from Adrea, she wouldn't have Chance. It was amazing what blessings God gave, even through horrible circumstances.

She regretted beginning Wade's tailspin, but she couldn't do anything about it. All she could do was share her blessing with Helen.

"Please sit down, Helen. I thought you might want to hold Chance, and I have wonderful news that will come as a bit of a shock."

"Okay." Helen sat in a rocker.

"Perfect, Chance loves to rock." She kissed his chubby cheek. "Remember Miss Helen I told you about? Do you want to go see her?"

With a grin, Helen reached for him.

Chance didn't shy away when Shell settled him in Helen's lap.

"What a friendly boy you are."

"He's used to being passed around at our church in Conway." Shell smoothed a curl away from his face. "Helen, I hope you won't be angry with me."

"Why would I be angry, dear?"

Shell took a deep breath and knelt beside Helen. "Because

you're just now getting to hold your grandson for the first time."

A gasp escaped and Helen's lips trembled. "Wade's son?"

"I'm so sorry." Shell's vision blurred. "I should have told you long before now."

Helen hugged Chance to her.

"It's okay, Chance." Shell patted his back. "Grandma Helen loves you. I told you she'd be excited to see you. She's crying happy tears and she's not trying to put you to sleep. No nap time."

As Helen took the hint and loosed her grip on him, he settled back in her lap making a rocking motion.

With a watery laugh, Helen rocked the chair. "Grandma Helen is very happy. Happier than she's been in years."

∂⸺

Ten a.m. Shell checked each house again. Ryler and Collin still gone. She drove the seven miles to Rose Bud. Cars had cleared out of the B & B. Down the road, Laken's car still wasn't home.

She'd have to head to Searcy. Thankfully, Helen had insisted Chance stay with her for as long as Shell needed. She'd wanted to take him with her, but what if things didn't go as planned? What if Ryler was still angry? Chance didn't need to witness any scenes and this one could go past his nap time.

Plans had already been promised for a picnic in the park tomorrow. And it sounded like Helen wanted to completely stop working at the florist and be at the B & B daily. No day care needed. It felt really good to make a lonely woman's day.

A red car met her. Hayden and Laken waved.

Collin's black Lexus was next, with him and Jill waving.

Any minute Ryler would be along. Last to leave because Sylvie wouldn't let go of him. With complete understanding, Shell thought of all the times she'd relinquished Chance to Savannah. Not anymore. *Lord, please help Chance easily adjust.*

Pulling onto the side of the road, Shell waited for a glimpse of a charcoal SUV.

A dark SUV came into view. She held her breath as it drew closer then huffed it out. Wrong model, navy blue.

Another dark SUV approached with a U-Haul on the back. Her breath caught. It was him.

Ryler slowed as he neared and pulled onto the shoulder across from her. He got out and jogged over. A deep frown marred his handsome features. "Car trouble?"

"You're moving?" Her voice quivered.

"I decided not to support the kind of landlord who gets his kicks by manhandling women, so I'm staying with Sylvie and Martin until I decide what's next. I'm headed back for the last load."

She blew out another big breath. "That'll be good for all of you. Make up for lost time and get to know one another."

"Martin's going into rehab for a month and Sylvie was nervous about being alone." He splayed both palms upward. "What are you doing here?"

"I met Laken and Collin, so I figured you'd be along soon. We need to talk. The B & B or the park?"

"The B & B." He ran a hand through his hair. "What's going on?"

"I'll tell you all about it there."

With a deepening frown, he jogged back to his SUV. He waited until Shell turned around in a driveway before pulling out behind her.

Her insides turned jittery. What if he'd changed his mind? What if she'd hurt him and he didn't want her? What if he didn't believe her about Darrell? *Lord, please work things out for us.*

She turned into the drive of the B & B and he followed. Her insides lurched as she stepped out of her car.

The green lush grass spread around the house like a carpet. Not a weed in sight. Roses and blossoms of every color surrounded each fountain, with benches in the midst and stone walkways leading to the house and the driveway. The miniature Romance Waterfalls splashed and trickled.

"Why didn't you ever plant anything at your rental house?"

"I never planned to put down any roots there."

Me neither. All she'd wanted was to finish the job and get out of town. Now all she wanted was to stay. With Ryler. Forever.

The balcony was empty. "Let's go up there."

"Sure." Ryler slowed his pace to match hers.

He strode to the porch, opened the arched-window door, and ushered her inside.

The clerk at the desk looked up. "Hi, Shell. Eva and Darrell are so relieved you're coming to manage this place."

Ryler's eyes widened.

"I'm excited, too. Nelda? Right? We're just going to borrow the balcony for a few minutes."

"That's fine. I think all our guests are out sightseeing."

Nerve endings buzzed with his nearness as Shell climbed the wide staircase and reached the landing.

Ryler opened the door to the balcony for her. "You're staying here?"

She perched on the swing and patted the seat beside her. "I brought Chance with me."

"Where is he?" Ryler shoved his hands in his pockets and remained standing.

"At Helen's, getting acquainted with his grandmother."

Ryler gasped. "I'm glad. She needed to know about him. I'm proud of you for doing the right thing."

"Me, too. She's so happy and Chance latched on to her. But I need to get back soon."

"So that's why you came back? For Helen."

eleven

"Sit down." She patted the seat beside her again. "Please."

He sat and drew an imaginary line between them.

Her laugh came out watery. "Remember when you asked me why I left when you wanted me to move in with you?"

"I'm glad you didn't now."

Closing her eyes, she swallowed hard, loving him so much it hurt inside. "You're not going to make this easy, are you?"

"That's not what I—"

"You said I was only looking for Mr. Right Now, but I found more than I was looking for."

"You did?" His gaze stayed firmly on the floor.

"In my experience, men don't stick around. So, I left before you did."

"Why'd you leave this time?"

She sucked in a deep breath. "Once I found out your blood was blue, I didn't think I was worthy."

"Blue blood? Me?" His laugh echoed sarcasm. "Talk about not being worthy."

"But we both are, don't you see? I just needed to hear it from a higher source." A yellow butterfly flitted about. Once a bumpy, wormlike caterpillar. Now a new creature. "Last Sunday, God told me I was worthy. Of Him and of you. Not directly, but through a Sunday school teacher. If Mary Magdalene can become a respected member of the community and Christ's inner circle, through His love, so can I."

"I tried to tell you that."

She shrugged. "I know, but I was too beat down by my mother, jerks, and snobs to hear it."

"I need to know about Darrell. What's going on there?"

Grabbing his chin, she forced him to look at her. "Nothing.

When I first moved to Conway, Darrell gave me a job cleaning apartments. His manager quit, so he trained me. Eva took me under her wing. If not for them, I'd probably be in some menial job, barely scraping by on minimum wage." Or following in her mother's footsteps.

"You crossed the line." He traced the imaginary line between them. "So Eva knows about you."

Shell bit her lip. "There's nothing to know about. Eva's an interior decorator and realized I had talent in that area. She mentored me and allowed me to design and decorate the clubhouse and condos when they bought the golf course in Searcy. And the whole time, they invited me to church and witnessed to me, but I guess I wasn't ready to hear it."

"What about that day at the roasterie? Did it really require you and Darrell, without Eva, to order coffee?"

"Eva was in the roasterie watching a demonstration." She rolled her eyes. "Do you really think that if Darrell and I were an item, we'd hang around together in public?"

Ryler's eyes squeezed shut. "So there's never been anything between you and Darrell?" A smile played over his lips and he turned them into her palm.

She shivered and her heart somersaulted. His gentle touch warmed her soul. "I spent my entire childhood watching my mother destroy marriages. A distraught wife even came to our house packing a gun and I think she'd have shot my mother if not for Savannah and me. Trust me, I would never get involved with married men. Besides, Darrell is one of the most honorable men I know and he's crazy about his wife."

"He treated you more honorably than I did." Ryler hung his head. "I'm sorry for accusing you of that. I didn't see Eva at the roasterie and when I saw you up here on our balcony with him at the grand opening, my old jealousy surfaced."

Our balcony. Her heart danced.

"And I'm sorry for the things I said about Chance, too. You've obviously always put his needs first. I was hurt and lashed out with angry words."

She traced his jawline with her fingertips. "Eva's been

running this place, but that was never their plan. They always hoped I'd stay here. I'm planning to. As long as that's where you'll be."

"What about Chance?"

"We'll work it out. Like you said once, I bet there are lots of landscaping jobs in Conway. I'm not going anywhere without you."

He turned her hand over and kissed the back of it.

"There's another reason why I left the first time."

"What's that?"

"I thought I could get over you."

He grinned. "But it didn't work."

"I love you, Ryler."

"Oh, Shell. We've wasted so much time." He leaned his forehead against hers.

"No more wasted time. I want you to meet Chance. With my sister and brother-in-law's blessing, I'm going to bring him to live with me. Slowly at first, only if he adjusts well, and I'm going to tell him who his mommy is. If it works, we'll talk about his daddy when he's old enough. I have to do what's best for him."

"I'm glad. A child should be with his mother."

She slid from the swing and knelt on one knee beside him. "Ryler Grant or Martin Rothwell Kroft Jr. or whoever you are, will you marry me?"

"I'll think about it, only if you'll drop the Martin Rothwell Kroft bit."

Think about it? Her heart crashed against her ribs as she tried to play along with his humor. "If you insist, Rothwell."

"Maybe you can call me that when I get on your nerves."

"You'll never get on my nerves."

"Even after sixty or seventy years?"

"Never. So, is that a yes?"

"There's just one little problem."

"What?"

"We don't have anywhere to live."

She certainly didn't want to live across the street from

Wade's old house where so many bad memories dwelled. "We need a fresh start, anyway. Darrell's letting me stay in the apartment/honeymoon suite until I come up with something permanent."

"I could live quite happily with you in a honeymoon suite. We'll figure out something permanent together. Maybe buy land and build a house."

Her heart sank. What about all his starting over and following the Bible's principles?

"I won't live with you, Ryler." Her voice quivered. "Not until after the wedding."

"I meant after the wedding." He kissed her hand. "I'm glad you never moved in with me. I want us to build our lives together, with God's blessing. I'll marry you on our balcony on the Fourth of July."

A relieved sigh escaped, but her eyes widened. "Less than a week away?"

"It's perfect because from the moment I first kissed you, Shell Evans, I've seen fireworks."

Her vision blurred. His lips sought hers and fireworks blasted through her veins.

❧

Hand in hand, Ryler walked Shell toward Helen's door. "What if he doesn't like me?"

"He'll love you and he's not shy. Savannah and Jake attend a large church, so Chance is used to being passed around by the entire congregation." Shell knocked.

Helen opened the door. The little towheaded boy Ryler had seen in Shell's framed picture clutched Helen's skirt.

Scooping him up, Shell kissed his chubby cheek.

"He was an absolute angel," Helen gushed. "The entire time. Reminds me of—" Her eyes watered. "Please, come in."

The humble little house was neat and tidy. Cozy, with pictures lining the walls. Chance favored the blond man in most of them.

Shell patted Helen's arm. "I was afraid he'd get fussy as nap time neared."

"Not a peep. Ryler, it's nice to see you."

"Thank you, ma'am." His gaze riveted on Chance.

"Chance, this is Ryler. My fiancé. That means we're getting married." Shell bounced the child up and down on her hip.

"Hi." Chance chewed on his fist.

"Hi." Ryler's vision blurred. Chance deserved a chance at a real family, at having a father who loved him. With this child, Ryler would make up for Shell's rough upbringing and the last lonely twelve years of his life. This boy would be loved by two parents.

"Congratulations." Helen hugged Shell then gestured them to the couch. "When's the happy occasion?"

"Independence Day."

Helen's eyes widened. "This Thursday?"

"Know any florists who could whip something up?" Shell smiled as Chance clambered over to Ryler's lap.

"I believe I do."

"See, he loves you," Shell whispered. "Just like his mommy does."

&

Standing in her favorite gold and cream attic bedroom of the B & B, Shell smoothed her hands down her dress. Never had she imagined she'd wear a white wedding gown with everything it traditionally signified. But in God's eyes, she was pure. And His opinion was all that mattered.

A knock sounded on the door.

"Ryler?"

"Eva said you wanted to see me." He opened the door, wearing a navy pinstripe tuxedo. The red tie and cummerbund set off his dark coloring.

And her heart. "Hey, handsome."

"Hello, beautiful." He pulled her into his arms. "In approximately two hours, we'll be on our honeymoon. Right here in this very room."

"I can't believe Darrell ran the guests out for the entire afternoon and appeased them with an extra night free. Especially on a holiday weekend. It's like a fairy tale. But I don't understand why we had to have the entire place." She giggled. "All we need is one room and we could have stayed in the suite."

"You'll see later. Speaking of fairy tales, Sylvie wants you to wear these." He fished a long box from inside his jacket and opened it to reveal a strand of pearls. "They belonged to my great-grandmother."

Shell's hand flew to her heart. "They're lovely."

"Not as lovely as you." He stepped behind her.

Holding her hair up so he could fasten the strand, she shivered when his knuckle grazed her neck.

It seemed like as good a time as any. Maybe he wouldn't get too mad. "I saw a lawyer the other day."

"Funny. Me, too." The pearls clasped into place.

"What for?" She turned to face him.

He fished an envelope from an inside pocket. "I want to adopt Chance."

Her vision blurred. "Oh, Ryler."

"He's part of you. I love him, Shell, and I want to be his father. Legally and in every sense of the word."

"I want you to be his father, too."

"Is that why you went to the lawyer?"

Shaking her head, she gulped a deep breath and grabbed the envelope from the dresser. "I had this drawn up."

Ryler unfolded the legal document and scanned it. "A prenup. You had a prenup drawn up without telling me?" His neck reddened.

She winced. "I knew you'd never agree."

"Why, Shell? I don't want this. You know I don't want this." His jaw clenched.

"I don't want anyone to think I married you for your money." *Especially not you.*

"Who cares what anyone thinks, other than God and us?" He ran a hand through his hair. "I thought you were past this unworthy business."

"I am. But I want you and everyone else to know that your money doesn't matter to me. That I love you. You know—

rich or poor, in sickness or in health. Just humor me."

He sighed. "Until death do us part. But that's just it, Shell. If it's until death do us part, we don't need this."

"I do." She kissed him. "Please don't be angry. Let's go get married."

She hurried to the landing to let Darrell know she was ready. Ryler hesitated a moment at the top of the stairs.

Her heart plunged to her toes. Surely, he wasn't angry enough to leave her at the altar.

"Ryler?" Uncertainty echoed in her voice.

"Don't worry." He descended and kissed the tip of her nose. "I'm not going anywhere, my stubborn bride."

Ryler winked then strode out to the balcony.

Blowing out a big breath, Shell's hands shook as she clutched her red rose bouquet.

"Relax." Darrell offered his elbow as the wedding march began. "You're supposed to enjoy this day."

The door opened and they joined Ryler standing with his best man, Collin. Savannah served as matron of honor. Chance fiddled with the satin pillow holding their rings and scattered crimson petals long after the music stopped. Guests stood between the house and the front garden.

Six red, white, and blue carnation bouquets lined the balcony with half-moon, gathered American flags fanning out underneath and white, silk wisteria cascaded from the railing.

Perfect. Everything was perfect. Especially the groom.

Pastor Grayson opened with prayer and read several Bible verses on marriage.

Facing one another, she and Ryler took turns reciting their vows. Tears blurred her vision as she promised her heart, trust, and future to the only man she'd ever loved.

"Do you vow to love and to cherish one another, for richer, for poorer, in sickness and in health, until death do you part?"

Gently, Ryler slid the ring on her finger. "I do."

Solid. Permanent.

She slipped the matching gold band on his finger. "I do."

"I now pronounce—"

"Wait." Ryler held up one hand then pulled the prenup from his pocket. "I can't do it, Shell," he whispered.

She gasped. Her heart took a nosedive.

Ryler turned toward their guests. "Friends and family, Shell is worried folks might think she's marrying me for the Kroft money, so she had a prenuptial agreement drawn up. But we're forever and this thing means we're iffy." He ripped the document in two and stuck it back in his pocket. "Now you know, as I do, that her heart is pure. Carry on, Preacher."

Grayson raised an eyebrow. "Y'all don't need to discuss this further?"

"No. Get to the husband and wife part. Let no man put asunder and all the good stuff."

Pastor Grayson looked at Shell.

She nodded, her heart welling with love. Ryler trusted her and made sure everyone else did, too.

"I now pronounce you husband and wife. What God hath joined together, let no man put asunder. Ryler, you may kiss your bride."

His heart-stopping kiss made her dizzy. Squeals and loud, rapid pops surrounded them. Shell jumped. Fireworks blazed flickering, gunpowder trails through the afternoon sky.

&.

Even after an hour of pictures on the balcony, in the various gardens, and around all four fountains, the guests still lingered as the reception wrapped up.

Ryler sighed. *Go home now. Please. Would love to be alone with my bride.*

"So." Ryler wrapped his arms around her waist from behind as she gazed at the miniature Romance Waterfalls in front of the house. "We've got the whole place to ourselves for two hours and the attic room for two more days."

She leaned back against him and he propped his chin on her head. "Per your request, the ringer is off, with the answering machine on, and the staff is gone, except for the cook who's available whenever we call. Eva's handling my duties once the other guests return."

"There you are." Darrell's voice came from behind them.

Ryler stiffened and turned to face him without letting Shell go.

"With the groom's permission, I'd like to hug the bride."

Ryler tightened his arms around her.

"Relax, Ryler. Shell's like a daughter to me, and I've got my own bride I'm still head over heels in love with after seventeen years."

"Sorry. Old habit." Ryler let go of her.

Darrell gave her a brotherly hug. "I'm proud of you."

"Thanks. Me, too."

"There's a clearing south of here. . ." Darrell gestured behind the honeymoon suite on the opposite side from the day care. "It's surrounded by oaks, sycamores, and wisteria vines in the spring. I thought Eva and I might build there someday, but she likes the city. So, if you both like it, we'd like to give you five acres as a wedding gift."

Like some charity case.

"We can buy it." Ryler's spine stiffened. "We planned to look for land."

"Relax." Darrell patted Ryler on the shoulder. "I know you can buy it. You're a Kroft. But Shell has always done a great job for me and she's never gotten a bonus. I like you, Ryler. You're an honorable man, and I know you'll be good to her. I'd like to give you both a gift. Or I should say, Eva and I would like to give you this gift. So, please take it."

Ryler knew Darrell was harmless. Even if he were interested in Shell, Ryler trusted her. But for almost a year, he'd considered Darrell a threat and old issues died hard.

"I don't know what to say." Ryler cleared his throat.

"Say thank you." Darrell offered his hand.

"Thank you." Ryler accepted the handshake.

"Now, don't take it if you don't love it. We've got a hundred and fifty acres here. If there's another spot you like better, let me know."

"Thank you, Darrell." Shell gave him a peck on the cheek.

Ryler didn't even flinch.

"You're welcome. Now, I'll round up my lovely bride and leave. Maybe the rest of the guests will take the hint."

❧

Shivers moved through Shell as Ryler inconspicuously nibbled on her ear.

"Stop it." She giggled. "That tickles."

"Do you think they'll ever go so we can get to the fun part? Why aren't they leaving?"

They'd made a point of rounding the entire house, speaking with each guest. Now back at the front waterfall, guests still milled about.

"They're probably waiting for us to go. Most brides and grooms don't honeymoon at the same place they have the wedding."

"You're right. I'll see if I can speed things along."

"Ryler! Don't." She grabbed his arm, fingers tingling at his massive bicep.

"Why not?"

"It's rude."

"It's rude for people to keep me away from my bride when I've lived like a Boy Scout for almost a year. Now we're legal and these people won't go."

"These people are our friends and family."

"Well, they're starting to smell like three-day-old fish."

He clapped his hands. "May I have your attention please? My lovely wife and I are going to say final good-byes to our families. Since we're honeymooning here, you can throw birdseed while we go inside and then feel free to go."

Laughter canvassed the crowd.

"Why didn't you just say so?" Collin hugged Ryler with a macho smack on the back.

"I think I just did."

Laken hugged Ryler, followed by Sylvie and a much steadier Martin. Each Kroft member hugged Shell, murmuring sincere welcomes into the family.

She scooped Chance up. "I love you and I'll see you in three days."

Savannah hugged her. As Jake took Chance from her, Ryler kissed her son's cheek.

"Okay, we're going inside now." He grabbed her hand, turned, and ran toward the house in a shower of birdseed. Fireworks blasted and the smell of gunpowder drifted overhead as the departing crowd cheered.

Ryler took her hand and they stepped inside.

As the door closed behind them, he clicked the lock in place and bowed. "My lady."

He scooped her up in his arms.

She laughed. "Ryler, what are you doing? We already crossed the threshold."

"I've really, really, really been looking forward to tonight." Cradling her, he growled in her ear. "For months and months on end."

She giggled. "Me, too."

"I want our first time—not our first time, but our first legal, right-in-God's-sight time—to be special." He carried her up the stairs in a flurry of white satin and lace, *Gone with the Wind* style.

Only she didn't fight him.

At the top of the stairs, he nudged the attic bedroom door open. The gold room. Her favorite. Just inside, he set her down.

Certain she'd swoon as his lips claimed hers, she clung to him and her heart raced for the only man who'd ever made her feel like a lady.

A Letter To Our Readers

Dear Reader:

In order that we might better contribute to your reading enjoyment, we would appreciate your taking a few minutes to respond to the following questions. We welcome your comments and read each form and letter we receive. When completed, please return to the following:

Fiction Editor
Heartsong Presents
PO Box 719
Uhrichsville, Ohio 44683

1. Did you enjoy reading *White Pearls* by Shannon Taylor Vannatter?
   ❑ Very much! I would like to see more books by this author!
   ❑ Moderately. I would have enjoyed it more if

   _____

   _____

   _____

2. Are you a member of **Heartsong Presents**? ❑ Yes ❑ No
   If no, where did you purchase this book? _____

   _____

3. How would you rate, on a scale from 1 (poor) to 5 (superior), the cover design? _____

4. On a scale from 1 (poor) to 10 (superior), please rate the following elements.

   ____ Heroine   ____ Plot
   ____ Hero   ____ Inspirational theme
   ____ Setting   ____ Secondary characters

5. These characters were special because? _____
_____
_____

6. How has this book inspired your life? _____
_____
_____

7. What settings would you like to see covered in future
   Heartsong Presents books? _____
_____
_____

8. What are some inspirational themes you would like to see
   treated in future books? _____
_____
_____

9. Would you be interested in reading other **Heartsong
   Presents** titles? ❑ Yes ❑ No

10. Please check your age range:
    ❑ Under 18   ❑ 18-24
    ❑ 25-34   ❑ 35-45
    ❑ 46-55   ❑ Over 55

Name _____
Occupation _____
Address _____
City, State, Zip _____
E-mail _____

DIGITALIS

Having left his military career to take care of his young daughter, former Marine Colton Neely finds himself adrift. Before long, he readily joins the black ops group Nightshade and falls for a woman named Piper Blum. Will Colton survive a new romance and a dangerous mission into the blackest of nights?

Contemporary, paperback, 320 pages, 5.5" x 8.375"

HEARTSONG
PRESENTS

If you love Christian romance…

$12.⁹⁹

You'll love Heartsong Presents' inspiring and faith-filled romances by today's very best Christian authors. . .Wanda E. Brunstetter, Mary Connealy, Susan Page Davis, Cathy Marie Hake, and Joyce Livingston, to mention a few!

When you join Heartsong Presents, you'll enjoy four brand-new, mass-market, 176-page books—two contemporary and two historical—that will build you up in your faith when you discover God's role in every relationship you read about!

Mass Market 176 Pages

Imagine. . .four new romances every four weeks—with men and women like you who long to meet the one God has chosen as the love of their lives…all for the low price of $12.99 postpaid.

To join, simply visit www.heartsong presents.com or complete the coupon below and mail it to the address provided.